Black Heart Cinnamon Jar

ANDY BRANNAN

Copyright © 2025 by Andy Brannan
All rights reserved

ISBNs:

978-0-9905191-3-3 Kindle
978-0-9905191-4-0 Paperback
978-0-9905191-5-7 Hardcover

No part of this publication may be reproduced, distributed, or transmitted in any form or by any means, including photocopying, recording, or other electronic or mechanical methods, without the prior written permission of the author, except as permitted by U.S. copyright law. For permission requests, email me@andybrannan.com.

The story, all names, characters, and incidents portrayed in this production are fictitious. No identification with actual persons (living or deceased), places, buildings, and products is intended or should be inferred.

Cover photo "Not Going Back"
by Andy Brannan

Published by A Bee

Visit the author's website, andybrannan.com

For my mother, Yvonne Brannan

Mom, I want you to read this book. I know you can't, but that doesn't stop me from wanting it. Perhaps, someday, I will read it to you—next to a mountain lake, or at that park behind the library, or even on the shore of the Pacific, to the rhythm of the surf and the melody of the gulls. In fact, I will. I promise you that. The whole thing, out loud, no matter how long it takes.
I just hope you're listening.

Contents

White Mouse and Charlie, Part I

1 | Recalling my Father 3

Seeking advice from a parent who is no longer with us is not actually as difficult as it sounds.

2 | White Mouse 9

Mortal enemies, brothers in arms, pitted against each other on a dreamscape battlefield.

Black Heart Cinnamon Jar

Pocket Spring 21

When water is precious, a flower is a rare gift – especially to a young girl who has never seen a real one.

The Popcorn Caper 39

Cathy and Ryan have a good time at the movies, despite a few minor inconveniences.

The Lost Lightning Bug 53

A young lady is starting to grow up, whether her father understands it or not.

Candy, Bags, and Purity 69

Sometimes a leap of faith is all we have. For Sasha, even a small chance for a new life seems worth any risk.

The Apothecary 81

Karly is on the right path, but sometimes there are things that must be set aside until the time is right.

Not Going Back 103

Carrie lands in a new place, determined to burn her bridges behind her.

The Black Heart 115

Mother had her Aunt Matty, and that's exactly who she needed.

White Mouse and Charlie, Part II

3 | Stops and Keys 137

In which Charlie wins the fight.

4 | Replacement Fuse 147

In which White Mouse gets the upper paw.

5 | The Lever of Possibility 161

In which a terrible threat reveals a new path.

6 | The Empty Cup 175

Reflections of an imaginary father fade into silence.

Rose of a Purple Thorn

Thorn 181

An unknown band of epicene musicians play a late-night show after the main act has left the stage, only to discover their new biggest fan.

Lagrange 193

Rowan and Hamsa find their romantic arts evenly matched in a space outside of binary norms.

Up Draught Coffee Co 205

Indy speaks his truth at poetry night, only to find a fellow spirit in mirror form.

War Trees 225

Cammie and Indy discuss the power of belief and sacrifice over coffee before jumping into the fray.

At Water's Edge 231

All of the baggage of the human mind and body dissolve in the moments before crossing beyond the shore.

Dreams of the White Farmhouse 237

Avery is haunted by recurring dreams of a mysterious house, but when they choose to seek help, they trigger sinister retaliation.

Once Upon a Time

> The Two Hedgehogs 255

For Mitch Tiner (10/31/1964 – 1/28/2021)

White Mouse and Charlie Part I

> *"There are two angels with a man—one of righteousness, and the other of iniquity"*
> *– Hermas, "The Shepherd," c 150 AD*

1 | Recalling My Father

I am not the kind of person to reach out for help. Yet, as days get longer and years become ever shorter, I find that I need my father more than I would have thought. More than I did as a child, and I think more than I did as a young man. When he passed away, I was well into middle age. I recall feeling a sense of liberty, a new potential, as though being free of his influence would allow me to paddle and drift at will upon a broad sea of possibility. Of course, I grieved as well. I carried a basket of regrets, guilt, and things I had forgotten to say, held like a bouquet I could never deliver. This is the natural order of things; the way it's always been done.

However, the day came when I needed a strong shoulder to lean on, and I had none. A lone wolf, I had rarely made close attachments, and the few I had tended to be self-sufficient, rugged individualists like myself. I felt that no support would be available, and that the very act of asking would be an affront to my stoic peers. I was raised in California by a Midwesterner, thus was my fatalist exterior tempered with a pronounced Golden State heart; a soft, chewy nougat buried under layers of dark, hard matter. I felt that I needed my father's wisdom, but he was not here.

So, I decided to recreate him from my own memories. I would visualize the man I knew, face him in my mind, and directly ask him for advice. I sat long hours, considering his words. Poring through our conversations, looking for patterns—remembering his cadence, his tone, his well-worn sayings. I thought about his jokes, his observations, questions, and authors he would frequently quote. I listed his favorite color, food, song, bird, car, house, river, tree, president, and several pages of book titles. I found his hat, stored for an age in an attic box, a lonely relic of a slowly balding head. I placed it before me and listened to him, once again, tell the story of how he'd found it, with new variations and plot twists creeping into each telling.

I recalled, as best I could, his descriptions of my mother, of whom I have no memory. Even as a small child, I missed this amazing woman I had never met. I knew her preferences in theater, her favorite pet, the way she laughed, and what she would say when she was ready for bed. I could almost smell her perfume, a gift from my father, when I looked at worn and creased photos of her, my dad's voice narrating each of them. He would describe her in great detail, and the things he chose to retell gave me additional insight into his own character.

I gathered my father from memory, assembled him, and asked him one question:

"Dad, I have always tried to live an honest life, to be a good person. I have always tried, but I've so often failed. I feel that there is part of me that refuses to submit to moral norms. It riles me against authority, pits me against my better self, and feeds my heartburn with the spice of greed. It often refuses to let me sleep, filling my head with doubt and shame. It wakes me up in the morning, buzzing with resentment for insults that haven't yet happened. How can I remain loyal to my values, when faced with this never-ending internal conflict?"

My father never answered a question right away. He would listen, nod his head, and sit in silence—sometimes for several minutes—before he replied. My imaginary version of him was no different. I could see his head dip slightly, several times, as I spoke. I could almost feel his hand reaching out to rest on my forearm or shoulder, or to pat my back. How could I think I didn't need this? And why could I never find such comfort in anyone else? Eventually, he spoke.

"There is an old Cherokee legend," he said, "which goes like this: A Cherokee man is teaching his grandson about life. 'A fight is going on inside me,' he said to the boy. 'It's a terrible fight, between two wolves. One is evil—he is anger, envy, sorrow, regret, greed, arrogance, self-pity, guilt, resentment, inferiority, lies, false pride, superiority, and ego. The other is good—he is joy, peace, love, hope, serenity, humility, kindness, benevolence, empathy, generosity, truth, compassion, and faith. The same fight is going on inside you—and inside every other person, too.' The grandson thought about it for a minute and then asked his grandfather, 'Which wolf will win?'"

My father stopped there. It looked as though he was finished.

"Well?" I asked, "Which one wins?"

"It depends on who you ask." A short, searching look, and he continued. "Some would say it's the one you feed, some would say neither, or both, I guess. It's just a story."

I was a little exasperated. "But the Cherokee must have passed the story down for a reason. What's the point?"

"Well, that's up to you. It's probably not even a real Cherokee story, anyway. It sounds like the kind of bullshit white people make up, then say it's Native American to make it sound profound."

My pretend father was exactly like the real one had been. Perhaps I did too well on this re-creation. I started to ask another question, but he stopped me.

"Son, I can't tell you what someone else thinks that story means, or what you should think. I can only say what it means to me. Think about the wolves fighting. For me, the point is the fact that it's a fight. How do I handle a fight? Do I cheat? Do I run away? Is it important to win? Can I make my opponent think they'd won? Whatever tactics I can use in a fight, I can apply to that struggle with myself."

"This is basically the allegory of the shoulder angels," I said, "or an angel and devil in the cartoons. In reality, it's much more complicated than all that."

My imaginary father looked at my face for a moment, then said simply, "Okay. Sure. Why don't you tell me what it's really like?"

I began talking.

2 | White Mouse

Charlie was, and always had been, the guardian of The Computer. We see him standing near the gold and platinum orbs and wheels of his charge, rearing up on his hind legs, alert, heroic. Charlie's sleek brown fur had a sheen that spoke of long, fastidious hours spent grooming, polishing his regal appearance, that none may doubt his dedication and professional ethic. His dark, dewy eyes were large, and all black, like a pair of smoky aviator's glasses floating above the whiskers that twitched now and then as he tested the air with his delicate and subtle nose. A mouse of his stature need only lift a paw and, reaching out, brush it casually against the sky, leaving streaks in the shimmering path of the harvest moon that swept past the colorless landscape of midnight.

But there were more important things to do. The Computer, it seemed, was about to wake up. Motors had begun to turn, with the whirring of tiny gears and large pullies. There was a tightening of cables, strung to spindles of glistening sapphire, spun with skeins of joy and pain, willfulness and woe, hopes, dreams, and vain regrets. This was the work of White Mouse, he knew. Charlie could see the pattern, like flickering neon and a cracked cobblestone path. In the same way that we can see the presence of wind in the distance through the waving of treetops or the rippling of water, we can see the presence of White Mouse in the unscheduled activity of The Computer.

Charlie directed his attention to the shadows of the periphery, seeking to ferret out any signs of movement. His ears, ample scoops like parabolic reflectors, tilted about, to the back, sides, and front—radar locators that sought the hidden enemy. He glanced over his shoulder, noting the lazy motion of his mechanical ward, somnambulant, idling in that space between reality and dream, as though life and death were merely the playthings of the lamentable White Mouse.

As guardian, our hero knew he would be the only defense. No one else would come, there was no one to call, no safety net. He was the barrier, the checkpoint, the fire line. Charlie must always balance the risk: he could remain at his post, awaiting the attacker that would surely show himself. Or he could take the offensive posture, venturing into the shadow to spar directly with the adversary, who would often bolt at the first sign of resistance. The devil, we know, is a coward, too afraid to earn an honest living, relegated to shadow and shame, shrinking before the Shield of Faith, and the Sword of Spirit.

On this night, the second option won out, and Charlie stepped away from the warm glow of the sleepy machine, toward the abyss of uncertainty that lay at the edge of the candlelight, where we can imagine all manner of circling eyes glinting out of the black. Just one brown mouse, proud and erect, feet spread in battle stance befitting the mightiest centurion, his back to the yellow wall of his innocent trust, stepping toward the point of the last, stealthy sound his tiny ears had detected. One step, then another, and after great deliberation, with a deep breath, a slow exhale, one more. Three steps were the limit, the greatest distance from the gate that tonight's suspicious context could warrant. Charlie remained there, straining to burn through the inky air with his equally black eyes, watching for the slightest movement, or any flash of white fur, rendered gray by the distant, narrow moon.

Sure enough, there was a soft, ever so slight stirring, at the very edge of perception. Slowly, a dusky blob faded into being directly in front of Charlie, exactly on level with his own face. The blob began to resolve, creeping out of the damp, oppressive air like a puff of steam, condensing into a long, pointed face, starkly white, with clear red eyes. The face continued to slide forward, stopping just outside of Charlie's reach, hanging motionless over a scrawny body of fuzzy snow. White Mouse never blinked. That was the thing about White Mouse: no blinking, no twitching of whiskers, no expression whatsoever. Just those facetless rubies, emotionless, with no visible sign of life, really, but somehow staring into your heart through the openings in your face, daring you to not blink in return.

This situation lasted eons. Or maybe it was only a second, it's quite impossible to say with any certainty. Charlie remained still, projecting resolve with each drop of breath, oozing fortification from every pore. It was a stand off, and White Mouse knew it. There would be no talking, no sound (there never was) but somehow the opposing forces, mouse to mouse, pata a pata, reached an understanding. It was in the air, with White Mouse declaring, "I'll be back," and Charlie rejoining, "I'll be ready." The angular, pallid face receded, like that of a drowning victim fading into the sea, and the tense night air began to breathe once more. Charlie turned, stepping back to his post, noticing The Computer was already spinning down to hibernation for the time being.

Charlie knew the moment had passed, and the dodgy nighttime prowling of White Mouse would be over, for now. He sat down, drawing his legs up into a pretzel shape that made him look more like Yoda than the Roman Guard of earlier, and began his meditation practice. "Defense is a game of the mind," he reminded himself. "There is no danger greater than those of attachment to the past or fear of the future." In Charlie's mother tongue, these words rang in a rhyming mantra, bold but smooth, like fresh summer honey on toast. He remained, trancelike, savoring the images of his relaxation.

The chirping of birds drew Charlie out of his reverie, back to alert status. He sniffed the air cautiously, finding all was well. The sun would rise soon. When it did, The Computer would boot to a world of birdsong over the vaporous meadow, and dancing shadows would echo the silhouettes of tall, dark trees framed in a sky of pale black and indigo pastel. Even now, there were clicking noises emanating from the lower structures of the mechanism. This—the measure of all things, the center of the known universe, the deep thoughts of all that is good, evil, neither or both—would start each day with a few quiet pops and crackles, like a campfire starting from bits of driftwood and dry grass.

But also like campfires, as in all things, there are good days and bad days. Sometimes, the crackling grows steadily, sending tiny tongues of flame like so many golden flower petals blooming to happy warmth, suitable for brightening the damp and dreary dawn of any fog-locked strand, easily controlled, simple to enjoy with a cup of tea and a scone. Other times, the entire campground could erupt in explosive blaze, showering the world around it in ravenous piranhas of fiery bolts, too many to stomp, too fast to outrun, too vicious to reason with, destructive creation on the hoof. Today was not the first kind.

The Computer ascended out of idle and into full steam in an instant. There was no interim period of contemplation, sitting around the breakfast table or even a simple yawn and stretch. The clicking noises just gave way to the revving of motors, grinding of gears, and swish of wind in the brassy path of chaotically careening planets in their eccentric orbits. Golden axles began to smoke, spinning furiously in gemstone bearings, while silver coils whined with the sudden release of so much pent-up energy.

The whole thing glowed with the power of an arc lamp, as though searching the entire sky with a single, immense beam. Charlie leapt to his feet, drawing his sword in a single motion as he rose.

It was too late. White Mouse had clearly been plotting this attack for some time. Charlie turned, attempting to face his attacker in vain. White Mouse at twelve o'clock—wait! Three o'clock! And six o'clock! Turning a full circle, he saw White Mouse at all hours, every cardinal point and intercardinal direction held the white, angular form of White Mouse, in legion, fully armed and poised for the strike. Staring blankly, expressionless, like words of no meaning, uttered by voiceless spirits in total silence, waking the dormant brain with meaningless philosophies, conflicts of no consequence, save the sinking, self-destructive wail of flat sails with all sheets unstuck.

"Defense is a game of the mind…" Charlie reminded himself, planting his feet, pressing his back into the hard iron slats of the gate. He held his sword vertically with the point tipped slightly toward the closest hostile element. He could hear the gears of The Computer singing behind him, but there was no looking over the shoulder now, or even the cupping of an ear in that direction. War was on, battle had begun, and the evil could not be allowed to prevail at any cost. "There is no danger greater," the litany helped Charlie focus, "than those of attachment to the past, or fear of the future."

Black Heart Cinnamon Jar

> *"I must confess that I think her as delightful a character as ever appeared in print, and how I shall be able to tolerate those who do not like her at least, I do not know."*
> – Jane Austen, letter to her sister, January 29, 1813

Pocket Spring

The weather service had predicted a pocket. It was the first in several years, and in Sarah's eye, every dome in the community seemed to tremble in electric anticipation. Deep down she knew that the shimmering was just the usual mirage effects of hot air rising carelessly from baked soil and dusty roadway, but still it was hard not to think that the dry, drab caps of the subterranean homes were excited for what was to come. Leaning her elbows on the thick casement of the dark, polarized vestibule window, Sarah craned her neck to peer at the sky for any sign of cloud. Nothing but the usual pale haze of atmospheric dust and traces of smoke from distant fires, through which the sun cast its yellow-stained rays on the golden mountains in the distance. The view resembled the tone of some ancient photograph out of a bygone era, Sarah mused. An era when there were real seasons, a regular living cycle. But now one could only hope for the occasional pocket.

"Amber!" Sarah called, "You and I have a little work to do."

"Work?" The seven-year-old appeared at the bottom of the stairs, curiosity in her small, dark eyes.

"Yes. And you know what?" Sarah descended a few steps down from the vestibule floor, paused for effect, then crouched, leaning forward a little and whispering, "You might even get to play outside!"

"Outside?" Amber was clearly confused. "In the daytime?" Her mother nodded. "Why would I want to do that?" Amber's brows were furled in concern.

Sarah was laughing now. "Outside! You'll see. But first we have a few things to take care of."

Sarah's laughter faded as she took on the calm, composed bearing of a mother who had set about carefully orchestrating a miracle for her child. She descended the rest of the stairs and, grabbing a stepstool from the kitchen, headed down one more level. Amber followed silently as her mother led the way into the pantry, where the light ducts cast the same sepia effect found outside. In this light, it could be difficult to tell one flavor from another (without actually reading the package) and more than once had this led to surprise food combinations at breakfast or dinner.

But Sarah didn't bother with the switch by the door, and with purposeful manner she planted the stool in the far corner and stepped up to balance on the highest tread. Even then, Sarah had to stretch, pawing about the top shelf for a few moments. Amber was transfixed. Something had gotten into mom, but the child couldn't determine what. Was there some emergency? No. Amber had seen her mother spring into swift action, with the stern-faced adrenaline of crisis. This was not that kind of urgency. Was mom going to show her a new game? No. This was a little bit like play, but too purposeful (and, besides, mom had said, "work to do.") This was something in between. A kind of happy emergency, perhaps. Something like that.

"Aha!" Sarah retrieved a small package from the dark recess of the back of the shelf and handed it to Amber. "These are just the thing."

Amber held the container reverently, having no idea what it could be, but sensing great importance in the treasure hidden away and revealed in such mystery. Her respectful poise, in contrast with her tousled hair, drew another giggle from her mother, now back at pantry-floor level.

"Okay. Come on." Sarah left the stepstool where it was and headed back upstairs.

In the kitchen, she had Amber place the package on the table. It was a coarse cloth bag, covering a box. It was perhaps large enough to hold a pair of shoes, thought Amber, or maybe only a single shoe. The box itself was plastic but appeared to be sealed with something. Amber watched as her mom began scraping it away with a small knife.

"It's wax." Sarah explained. "These have to be kept absolutely dry. We expose the open box to the sun for a little while, then close it up and seal it to make sure there is no moisture at all. They can last many years that way."

For Amber, the explanation created more questions than it answered. She remained silent, though enthralled by the process unfolding in the kitchen. Elsewhere in the house, games were waiting patiently to be played. There were things to read, and sounds to listen to, recordings of far-away breezes and crashing oceans. There were colors which could be moved about with little sticks, inviting the creative genius of the child mind. Downstairs, Amber had a collection of faceless dolls that only came to life in her hands. There were puzzles that changed patterns in weird, wonderful ways, and brainteasers that looked easy, but were not. Amber had a tree of lights in her playroom, with spectacular pulses dancing to the rhythm of centuries-old compositions, or flickering with new whimsical music one could make up on the spot. All of the voices that whisper the language of life into the growing mind of a child.

As Amber sat with her mother, there were yet races to run in the deep basement, and bicycles to ride through simulated landscapes. Amber could flip through images of faraway places, sometimes to tell made-up stories about them and the history she imagined must have created them. On most days, either Amber or a friend would make the brief, intense trek between homes, and they would play or have schooling, depending on the calendar. Hidden under her bed, Amber had a box of jewelry (which she thought was secret) and every so often she would open it up to remind herself of the times and places tied irrevocably to each bauble. There were so many things to do in the house, so much to draw a child's attention, all forgotten in the moment of wonder at this small, simple box of glorious mystery on the kitchen table.

It was open now. The inside of the box smelled like starlight, rust, parchment and time. Sarah gently lifted the lid, revealing neatly placed rows of small envelopes. There were lots of them. Amber wanted to dump them all out, to read the labels, and figure out the pictures that were printed on each. However, the process was to be drawn out in a fashion more deliberate than all that. Sarah flicked through them with her thin fingertips for a few moments and pulling one tiny packet from the bunch, handed it to Amber. "Do you know what this is?" she asked.

Amber looked it over. She could read the label, and the faded picture was clearly some kind of plant. Amber had seen other pictures of plants, of course, but she was having a very difficult time rationalizing what she knew about them with this little paper packet. Amber could feel the slight bulge of some lumpy contents, and a small shake elicited a dry rustling from inside—a fairy voice from a forgotten novel. She looked up at her mom, and asked, "Is this made from a plant?"

Sarah stifled a sob. Her eyes began to tear up. "Radishes, honey." She sniffed. "They're seeds, Baby Girl. We are going to plant them, and if we're lucky these will become radishes."

* * *

The clouds were beginning to show in the sky over the hot, arid August morning. By afternoon, they were gone, but the brief spectacle of atmospheric moisture was the expected omen. Like fluffy trumpets, the herald angels of an impending climatic miracle. The pocket was coming, and soon. Mother and daughter watched the patterns developing, hoping to get the timing right. Amber claimed she remembered rain, once. Sarah doubted that she actually did. The girl had only been three back then, and it was a single, brief downpour. The temperature had not even changed, really. It had been well in the dangerous range of heat, foggy for a few minutes, and humid for several hours afterward. Just because Amber talked about how awful that part was didn't mean she remembered it. She'd certainly heard others talking about it since, creating the memory she didn't really have. But this was going to be different.

The evening before the pocket, Sarah led Amber out to the north side of the vestibule. "This spot will give our garden enough shade to keep it from drying out too fast," she explained. "Even so, we will need to put some cloth down, and a cover after the pocket, to keep them going as long as possible."

After the sun was completely down, a breeze started up. It was a cool breeze: another tell of the pocket's onset, and a phenomenon completely novel to the child. Sarah and Amber removed their sun cloaks and began to dig. They turned the soil and prepared rows for the seeds. In other places, they prepared small mounds for those they had pre-germinated. They placed small markers to identify which crops were in each tiny patch. Then Sarah unfolded a large cover, painstakingly pieced together from burlap sacks she'd saved from the bulk dry goods delivered to the resource hub. They laid this cover carefully over the entire garden area, with stakes and rocks to hold it in place. But no seeds yet.

In the morning, Amber awoke to her mother's gentle prodding. "Let's go outside." Sarah turned and walked out of the room. Amber could hear an odd sort of rushing murmur in the distance. In her sleepy mind, she wondered idly what the sound could be, while in her waking heart she could feel the pounding footsteps of ancient ancestors, running free in forests and green fields, buzzing with life. She rubbed her eyes, got out of bed, and a few minutes later met her mom in the vestibule. The girl reached for her sun cloak. "You won't need that." Sarah said, smiling.

Amber was startled, but faithfully followed her mom out the door.

It was raining. It was cold (by Amber's standards), and the world smelled funny. They walked a few steps into the rain and stopped, a few yards from the front door. They both stood there in the rain, as though the world had just now presented itself for their first scrutiny. Amber looked up, blinked her eyes. She reached her hand into her hair, now soaked by the cool, soft drops, and pushed it behind her ear. She turned her small, thin face up at Sarah, who pointed. Amber looked to find that neighbors, down the street as far as she could see, were doing the same. Some were looking around, some were laughing, some were now hugging each other. Small children looked afraid, clinging to the legs of their parents.

Older people had gathered cups, tubs, and even wheelbarrows to capture some of the free water. A few seemed to be crying—in pain or joy—but the tears were masked by the flow of water coming in buckets from the dark, fluffy heavens. Amber turned back to her mother and started a squeal of joy that quickly resolved itself to a wordless song, and the dancing began.

Children ran between houses, while parents walked casually down the lane. Some had never seen each other's faces, and all greetings became happy introductions. Rivulets formed along paths and between houses, so the children responded by jumping across – back and forth, forth and back. A few were seen standing with arms and mouths wide, catching raindrops on tongues dry from years of oppressive futility, and smacking lips whose cracks were healing moment by moment. Sarah saw a little boy stomp in a mud puddle and wondered how he knew to do that. It took several hours for the initial bout of frolicking to die down enough for Sarah to divert Amber's attention to the garden. The pocket itself was expected to last two full weeks. There would be plenty of time to play later, after the work was done.

They planted seeds of several kinds. Sarah would pick a spot and poke a hole in the burlap with the slim blade of a long knife. Amber would follow behind, dropping seeds in the holes, following the labels they had set the night before. They planted green lettuce, bok choy, spinach, and arugula. There were cress, sunflowers, and beans, which would be harvested as sprouts. Bulb greens of chives, green onions, and scallions. They planted an entire section of herbs: fennel, dill, oregano, chervil, mint, coriander, chives, parsley and basil, some of which might be ripe enough to harvest when the time came. And, of course, the radishes. In a time and place where all vegetables were dried, canned, processed into extracts or made into other things, Amber had been looking forward to these the most.

Her mother had described radishes to her a week ago in the kitchen. "They're like water," she'd said, "only round, crunchy, and ruby red. Bright white on the inside, too, like a small light in a dark room. They don't have a flavor, so they go with anything or everything. But also, they do have flavor. They taste like the fondest memories of loved ones and happiness." After a pause, she added, "My mother showed me how to grow them, long ago, just like we're going to do." Amber was all in for the radishes.

Once all the seeds had been placed into the ground, Sarah held her hand out to the rain for a few moments, rinsing her muddy palms. Then she retrieved something from her pocket, and held it out to the girl. "One more thing to plant, Amber." In her hand was a small jar with what appeared to be a wadded up scrap of cloth. "These are nasturtiums." Sarah smiled at her daughter's quizzical expression. "They're a type of flower, Honey."

Amber looked at them in awe. "Flowers?" she asked, "we have flowers?"

"My mother gave me the seeds," Sarah explained, "quite a lot of them, actually. Every year, I take a few out, and I get them wet. Yes, I know, we are not permitted to use house water on plants, but this is only a few drops. I do this because some seeds take a long time to germinate— er, to get ready to sprout. During a pocket, there is just no time, and we would never, ever have these if they weren't prepared. So, every year, I take out a small number of seeds, start them with a tiny bit of water, put them in the refrigerator, and wait. Most years, their time runs out and I must throw them away." Sad notes hung in the damp air as the two women kneeled together by the garden, as if in melancholy prayer for the lost souls of the nasturtiums who had never made it. But Sarah continued. "This year," she said, "we have a pocket. These seeds are ready, and I think the timing is right. They have a chance!"

With that, she poked the planting knife through the burlap, and dropped a seed through the hole, into the dark, warm, welcoming soil beneath. They took turns, planting the seven seeds in silence. Amber looked up at her mom, and started to speak, then stopped. Sarah understood instantly. "You're done. Run and play! Go see the neighbors, with no sun gear! Enjoy it while it lasts!"

Two weeks to play in the rain. Two weeks for the water from above to bathe the tiny sprouting vegetables. Allowing for another week or two of growth after, Sarah felt that there would indeed be a small harvest before the soil hardened to cracked concrete under the merciless sun and plants became impossible once more.

***

The pocket broke on a Sunday. Amber didn't notice the irony of "Sun" for a "sunny" day, but she was astonished when the clouds parted to reveal a crystal clear, deep blue sky. Yes, the temperature was already rising, but the clean air, the dust-free lanes between the shining domes of the residential vestibules which dotted the community, the sparkle of the rooftops that could be seen on the resource hub and civic buildings in the distance—all of this was a new, uncharted world to Amber. She wondered: How long it would stay like this? Would the skies return to their normal brown color? Or would they stay this disconcerting shade of blue? Would this thing happen again? Another pocket—maybe this year? Further reflection was cut short by her mother's low voice. "Come on," she said, eyeing the retreating clouds. "We have work to do."

Sarah led Amber to a trap door leading to one of the out-basements. Near the bottom of the stairs, Sarah had staged a largish roll of white plastic, and a stack of longish tubes. Amber's questions regarding their purpose were answered when she and her mother began assembling them at the garden. They used these things to construct a pair of tents covering the plot, whose tiny plants were just beginning to break the surface.

"We won't be able to go inside these for more than a few minutes once it warms up," Sarah said. "It will be extremely hot and humid, at least for a week or two. Then it will just be hot and whatever's left in here will be dead. I'll keep an eye on it, and harvest just before that happens."

Amber had already turned away to gaze at the purple mountains in the distance. "Mom…?" she asked, "What is that?"

The girl was pointing at something, to an area of the plains some distance from the community. It was a patch of green, amid the dark sea of mud that was already starting to bake into the familiar tawny shade of the surrounding flats.

Sarah smiled. "I'd forgotten about this part. Or perhaps I didn't want to get my hopes up." She paused. "Those are plants, honey. Keep an eye on them over the next few days." She smiled and headed inside.

* * *

Early one morning, Amber awoke once again to a soft nudge from her mother. "Let's go outside." Sarah turned and walked out of the room. The little girl rubbed her eyes for a few moments before she realized what must be going on. She got out of bed, and a few minutes later met her mom in the vestibule. Mother and daughter ventured out into the pre-dawn darkness, with flashlights and baskets. The soil that had been turned to mud during the pocket was now very dry, crunchy, and peeling up at the edges between cracks. Together, they lifted the row covers from the garden.

They were met by a lush patch of green leaves, happily growing from the carefully curated oasis in the desolate ground of the community. Sarah and Amber harvested the greens, the bulbs, the sprouts, herbs, and the much anticipated radishes. Nearly everything seemed far enough along to eat. At the far end, amidst a small array of round, green leaves, were a few pale yellow buds. The nasturtiums were just starting to open, revealing the deep orange flowers that were coming into being.

"Do we pick them?" Amber asked.

Sarah paused in consideration. "Well," she said, "we have a choice to make." Amber, cued into her mother's contemplative tone; let a moment pass with no interruption. Sarah continued. "We could pick the nasturtiums now, and they would probably finish blooming in the house. We could even eat them."

"Wait, you can eat these?"

Sarah laughed, "Yes, we can. However, there would be no seeds to replace the ones we planted."

Amber was visibly trying to work out the importance of this. "Seeds… to grow more? You have more seeds, right?"

Sarah smiled, with a touch of sadness. "Yes, I do. However, once those are gone, there will be no more in this house. The line will be gone, and we will probably never see anything like them again. If we leave these plants here, the flowers may develop long enough for seeds to mature. Of course, they will dry out very soon in the heat. But if we put the cover back on, there's a chance that the seeds will survive, even as the flowers are dying. Then we could dry them and store them for some future day."

Amber had been eyeballing the plants. "How come there are only five?"

Sarah hadn't noticed, but her daughter was right: only five of the seven they had planted had grown. "Well," she explained, "not all of the seeds will grow. You plant them, and some make it. Others just don't. That's why the plants have so many – so there will be a better chance for new plants to start from their seeds."

Amber nodded, still thoughtful. "How many seeds are in each flower?"

"Mmm… three or four, I think."

"So," Amber had obviously come to a conclusion, and now offered a plan. "How about this: We cut one plant, and we'll have the flowers from that. The other four plants all have several flowers on them, so there should be…" (wheels turning) "I don't know, but a lot of seeds!"

"I see at least four flowers on some of the plants, and that one has six." Sarah walked through the arithmetic out loud, for emphasis. "That means there are more than sixty seeds to come, if there are any at all, probably more. Would you like some flowers?" Amber nodded vigorously; Sarah continued. "I say we pick two plants, and we can each have a bouquet."

"A what?"

Sarah laughed. "A handful of flowers, in a vase. You've seen pictures."

They continued laughing lightly as they replaced the row covers, and the eastern horizon began to glow.

They were carrying the baskets back to the house, when Amber spotted color in the distance, out in the plains. Sarah saw it, too, and paused, turning to her daughter. "Do you know what that is, Amber?"

Amber stared into the warm twilight air, straining to see some detail, but could only make out some areas of purple and a few yellow blotches. "The green patches—are those flowers, too?"

"Wildflowers, Honey." Sarah sat down on the ground, gesturing to Amber. "The seeds stay in the ground, waiting – sometimes for years. Just waiting for spring."

The Popcorn Caper

Cathy was cold. Her hoodie had gotten slightly damp when her parents had dropped them off, the relentless rain between the car and lobby pelting them as they ran. And now the theater seemed to have the air conditioning on. "Why is there AC?" she asked Ryan who was seated next to her. "Do they not realize it's cold out?" She was laughing to cover her annoyance. It was partly at being chilly, but she was also irritated with the theater, who might be sending this first date off to a bad start with their environmental settings. Ryan didn't seem overly concerned but sympathized right away.

"Mebbe there's a thermostat in here," he shrugged, "...if you want to mess with it."

"Yes! Yes, I do."

They made eye contact, each seeking to interpret the other's facial cues and body language. Was she kidding? Or did she want to risk the wrath of the ushers in adjusting the temperature? Was he serious? Or had he just thrown out a bad idea, expecting her to sit still and bear the cold? They were pretty early, and theater number five was still empty. The time was right, and they wanted to go get some snacks anyway. Cathy and Ryan each decided the other was up for a mini adventure, and stood in unison, leaving their damp hoodies to mark their seats.

They found what they were looking for near the door of the theater: a small white box on the wall marked "Honeywell," with the tiny rows of slots in the top and bottom—vents for air to pass over the sensor. Cathy looked it over, tugged at the edge tentatively, while Ryan peered over her shoulder, occasionally glancing at the door, keeping watch.

"I don't see any buttons," she said, "and it doesn't open."

Ryan pursed his lips and sighed. "I bet it's a slave unit," he speculated. "Like, the controls are somewhere else."

"Yeah, they wouldn't want customers making themselves comfortable, would they?" Cathy had a wry smile that seemed to say she hadn't given up yet. But she shrugged, saying, "Let's see what's at the snack bar."

As they stood in line, Cathy found herself wondering what movies people were here to see. Were those people here for an action movie? Adventure? That couple was holding hands; had they come out in the rain for a romantic comedy? Was the nerdy looking D&D type guy here to watch a sci-fi alone? Or did he have a date waiting with their seats? Who else was here for the anime, like her? This was one of Cathy's favorite movies, and she was very much looking forward to seeing it on the big screen. Ryan had never seen it but seemed willing enough to check it out.

Cathy's mind veered in a new direction. What if he didn't like it? Wouldn't that say something about him? What happens then? Do we need to decide today whether to have a second date? Would she want to date someone who hated her taste in movies? Would he want to date her again after dragging him to a lame show? Does one need to explain to friends at school exactly why it didn't work out? Dating sucks. I don't even know why I did this in the first place.

Her self-talk was interrupted by a tap on the shoulder. Ryan was pointing at something to the right of the snack counter. Cathy spotted it: a panel on the wall near one of the registers. It had a few buttons on it and a small screen. She could just make out the red Honeywell logo across the bottom, and she immediately realized what it was. "Of course!" She giggled, "They put the controls where we can't get at them!"

Ryan was laughing, too. He was tall, imposing for a teenager. His flannel shirt made him look like a cowboy, but the Vans on his feet said he'd more likely be seen on a skateboard than a horse. Of course, he did work at a ranch supply store, so perhaps his western look had developed there. He spent the days stacking bags of grain, bucking hay bales, loading trucks with fence panels and water troughs. His deep tan showed he had been working at it all summer; his rough hands showed he still was in the fall.

Cathy wanted to learn more about him. Of course, she knew him from school, but they had not talked until very recently, as they had mainly been interacting with separate crowds. But high school was mixing people up in new combinations, with old friendships fading and new ones forming. The girls Cathy hung out with these days were the latest version of a group that had started forming in middle school, but now had become a fulltime posse. Yes, they would be asking about this date, since they had pressured her into going in the first place. But did she have anything to say? Cathy couldn't decide.

They were nearing the front of the line. Cathy looked at the thermostat controls on the wall, wistfully considering throwing herself on the mercy of the staff, requesting a manager, begging them to change the temperature. But Ryan had other ideas.

"Get ready," he said. "While they're distracted, you run to life support, set it how you want!" He was pointing at the panel.

"Wait, what?" she asked, but it was too late.

Ryan stepped out of line, casually walking to the end of the counter. Nobody was watching him. He paused for a moment, waiting for the right time to…what? Get their attention somehow? He didn't seem to be placed right for it.

Cathy was not prepared for what happened next. Ryan glanced at her, and with a nod, he ran behind the counter. Before anyone could react, he had grabbed a large bucket of popcorn and took off down the hall! At first, he was just walking fast, but as the entire crew dropped what they were doing and started after him, he sped up, shoving handfuls into his mouth as he periodically glanced over his shoulder. Now he was laughing manically, a trail of popcorn behind him; he ditched down a fork in the main hall and kept going.

Cathy looked around. The counter was deserted, all staff had become nothing more than muffled shouts receding in the distance with Ryan. She walked quickly past the other customers. They mainly stood there laughing, phones in hand, hoping to get some video of this crazy guy getting arrested and dragged from the building, kicking and screaming, maybe biting people—who knew? In any case, nobody seemed to notice her as she stepped up to the climate control panel, looked it over, and quickly figured out how to set the temperature. The display changed to reflect that heat was now running in the theater. Cathy retreated, back to the queue.

The video-ready bystanders were greatly disappointed when Ryan returned, a free man, laughing with the small knot of staff members who were now sharing popcorn with him. Cathy was astonished. Part of her had expected him to get kicked out of the theater at the very least, and she was in the process of deciding whether she should go back in and watch the movie alone. But here he was, none the worse for the experience, and holding a now mostly empty bucket of popcorn as he approached. Coincidentally, it was their turn.

Ryan paid for the popcorn, while Cathy ordered drinks for both of them. On top of everything, Ryan asked for a refill, since the largest size is a bottomless bucket of popcorn. This got a few more laughs, since much of the contents was actually strewn about the hall, but no one seem to object. She saw her date leave a nice tip on the counter for the crew, then the two of them walked back toward the theater. As soon as they were out of earshot, Cathy leaned close, whispering, "What the fuck, Dude!" She was trying not to explode in laughter. "Why didn't they kick you out?"

"When they caught me at the far end," Ryan explained, "I offered them some popcorn, and told them I'd pay for it. Showed them the cash, to prove it."

"That's it? Just, 'Oh, my bad, I have money…'?"

"Well," Ryan's tone was now confiding, "I may have told them you dared me to do it."

Cathy finally could not contain her amusement. She was cracking up as they entered their theater, nearly shouting, "So that made you a folk hero, or what? Jesse James, outlaw popcorn thief!"

"Shhhh!" Ryan suppressed a snort, "We're in the theater!"

"Oh, yeah," Cathy was now whispering, "Shhhh - quiiiiiiet!"

They got back to their seats only moments before showtime. The theater was still empty.

"Where is everybody?" Cathy was perplexed. It was a well-known movie, popular with the anime crowd. While a small turnout might be expected on the screening of an older show, there should at least be a few fans. "Odd."

Once the feature had started, Ryan and Cathy settled in to watch, munching popcorn, sharing an armrest. It did not take long before Cathy noticed a new wrinkle: the movie was in Japanese, with subtitles.

"Oh my god." She was reaching for her phone, now looking for the ticket screen. Yep, it said so right there. "Okay, they show these for only a few days, with most of the shows in the English-dubbed version." Ryan nodded. Cathy continued. "Some showings, just a few, are in the original Japanese." She looked up at her date, aghast. "I didn't notice which one this was when I bought the tickets!"

Cathy was on the verge of tears. She suddenly wanted this date to go well. Ryan had started to seem very attractive, and the embarrassment of the situation was becoming physically painful. Ryan, sitting tall in his seat, was smiling down at her, which seemed to help the mood.

"I don't speak Japanese," he said, "but I have a great playlist." He held up his phone. Cathy did not see a connection between these two facts, and her expression must have said so. "You have a set of earbuds, right? Let's pair 'em and share 'em."

And that's exactly what they did. One ear to the right, and one to the left, they settled in to watch a spectacular world of hand-drawn color sliding across the screen to the sound of Japanese voice actors and American songs. Ryan's selection of music was perfect, filled with mostly familiar tunes and artists that Cathy loved. The theater was no longer cold. This was thanks in part to the change in the thermostat, but lifting the armrest and leaning into each other didn't hurt, either. Neither of them really cared about the subtitles anymore.

Sometimes in a dark theater a boy might slip his arm around the shoulder of his date. In fact, this happens quite a bit. A girl might lean into him, and sometimes she does.

The boy might wonder what she's thinking, and she might wonder the same. Or she might be watching the movie—who knows? A girl might put her hand on the knee of her date because it seems comfortable, and he may or may not respond to that. This sort of thing can go on for an entire movie in the darkness of the theater.

Ryan's off-hand rested gently on Cathy's forearm. She liked the feel of his rough, calloused palms and his strong fingers. The movie was about half over. Cuddling with her date, she was happy. She felt his other hand moving slightly, where it draped down her side. She hadn't really noticed much as Ryan had placed his arm around her, but now the slight tickle against her ribs drew her attention. His hand drifted a bit, rising up to touch the bare skin near her collarbone.

Cathy's stomach leaped. She was not surprised with Ryan, but she was having some trouble sorting herself out. The feeling was like hot cocoa on Christmas when she was five, only warmer and more chocolaty. She recalled another time, handling a baby bunny at a friend's house—her ten-year-old heart going pitter-patter with the fuzzy touch, the floppy ears. This was like that, too, but a hundredfold. Butterflies. That's what this was called. She'd heard it somewhere, in a song or something. Yes, definitely butterflies, in the best possible way.

Ryan's hand had followed her clavicle toward the center of her chest, where it began toying with her top button. As he did so, his fingertip dipped inside her blouse slightly, only at the edge, near the top, but just a teeny bit under the fabric. The butterflies became a wave, covering a sunset beach in a gentle, glistening sheen, rising and receding moment by moment. The feeling grew, until it became a riptide, pulling Cathy away from the shore. Exciting, energetic, but startling, frightening at the same time. She sat up a little straighter, raising her hand to Ryan's, still not sure if she was about to invite him in or block him. He froze.

Cathy's voice managed somehow to start out clear and firm. "Just because you risked your life for me with the popcorn caper," she exaggerated a little, "does not entitle you…" Cathy trailed off at that point, trying to make out his face in the darkness.

There was an exceedingly long moment of waiting, perfectly still, two statues in a gallery of uncertainty. Then, the scene on screen changed, with brighter colors that lit up the room. Cathy could see a flash of anger in Ryan's eye, and she recoiled just a bit.

So did Ryan, at the same time pulling his arm back, leaving Cathy's close personal space. It was only seconds later that he spoke up.

"I'm sorry." He said, "I just thought…" Now he was the one trailing off, and Cathy could hear in his voice that the irate look she had seen was fleeting, and possibly even embarrassing to him.

He grabbed the popcorn from the neighboring seat and began munching on a handful. Cathy decided to make this move a bit ironic, saying, "You haven't even kissed me yet. You need to stay in your lane until you get where you're going!"

"Wait," mumbling through a mouthful of popcorn, "I wazh shuposhed to kish you?"

"Maybe. Guess we won't find out." She paused, then added, "And don't even try it with food in your mouth!"

They both chuckled a little, then got distracted by the action on the screen. Before long, they were cuddling again, enjoying the music and movie together much as before. Then it was over, and they gathered their things, heading for the lobby. After texting their parents, they waited inside the glass doors, staying warm until their ride showed up. Ryan noticed that he was still holding the popcorn bucket. He held it out.

"My gift to you," he said.

"Thanks!"

"It's refillable."

"Yes, it is." Cathy was tempted to run up to the counter and fill it right then, but there was a line.

"You know…" Ryan started to speak, then paused.

"Yes, I know."

Ryan laughed. "No, you don't! You don't even know what I was going to say!"

Now Cathy was laughing. "Does that matter? I never said what I know, either!"

Still laughing, Ryan said, "Brilliant!" then added, "I could kiss you!" It was in much the same playful tone as one would say, "You're so awesome!" or "Thank you very much!"

Cathy met his gaze directly and said, "Yes, you probably could." She grinned, and added, "Maybe next time."

The ride was outside, the moment was cut short. Cathy had been holding Ryan's hand in hers, but now dropped it in favor of the empty popcorn bucket, holding it over her head as they ran through the rain to the car.

The Lost Lightning Bug

Part 1: Abigail

Gail was bored. It was still only July, and (as crazy as this sounds) she was already beginning to look forward to seventh grade. Not that she minded school so much, really. It's just that she had expected more from summer. What had she done last year? Gail couldn't seem to remember exactly what it was, but her summer had not been like this, she was sure of it. There was the county fair, of course. That was coming up in three days. It would probably be as much fun as it was last year. And there were few trips to see the cousins, a tradition which was about the same this year as last. Yet Gail still felt that this was the slowest, emptiest, boringest summer ever. She just wanted it to be over.

The sun had set, and Gail decided to go out to the pond. Perhaps the fireflies would be out. In fact, they probably would be. She packed a basket with provisions: a few cookies, a small mason jar of milk, her flashlight, and a shawl. There was an old wooden bench by the water, where she sat down to have her snacks. Sure enough, the lightning bugs were flitting about in the reeds along the edges of the placid water. There were quite a few tonight, with nearly continuous flickering spreading out around the shore, the mirror surface doubling the effect. Believing the house was far out of earshot, Gail began to sing to the tiny glowing insects. She made up songs full of flowers and honey, cookies and milk, spring and fall.

As she sang, she unconsciously began flicking the button on the flashlight, keeping the rhythm to her mildly silly verse. This went on for several minutes. Singing softly, flashing the light, a sort of soporific meditation in the diminishing warmth of the summer evening. After a while, Gail noticed that a few of the fireflies had flown over to her. They were quite near, in fact. This was something new! As an experiment, the girl turned the flashlight completely off and watched. The lightning bugs slowly meandered away, back to their grassy homes.

How interesting! Gail finished the last of the milk and cookies, then began flashing the light once more. Several fireflies, indeed, made their way in her direction. After a few more experiments, it was clear that this was a thing:

the bugs were definitely attracted to the glow. It was a very short leap of logic to reach the conclusion that, if these things were easily called, they could be easily caught. A few minutes later, Gail had determined that she could coax a firefly to land on her shawl, which was now draped over her arm. From there it was a simple matter of scooping it up in the empty mason jar.

"Daddy! Daddy! Daddy!" She had abandoned everything at the bench and was running to the house with the jar. "I've got a lightning bug! I got one, I GOT one!" Dad was already at the back door, holding it open for her as she blazed through the pantry into the kitchen. "I'm naming him 'Rodney'," she announced, her face beaming in obvious joy. "But we can call him 'Rod'," pausing. "Lightning Rod. Get it?"

Dad laughed at the joke, and admitted it was a fine name. "We need to poke some holes in the top, so it has some air. Okay?" About that time, mom came onto the scene, wondering what the commotion was about. She stood assessing the situation for a moment.

"Abigail," her mom began. "Are you sure you are ready to keep a pet? Do you know how to take care of a glow worm?" Gail stopped what she was doing for a moment, and said, "First, Rod is a lightning bug, not any kind of worm. Also, he isn't a pet. He's my friend! And I think Rod and I can figure it out." She turned to Dad. "I'm calling Kelli. Can Kelli come over?"

Thus began an impromptu sleepover, with Gail's best friend Kellianne. Really, Kelli was the only school friend Gail had seen much of during the summer, being the only one who lived nearby. The two girls disappeared into Gail's room and were not heard from again that night. After breakfast, Kelli stayed around most of the morning. There was talk of catching more fireflies, but Gail was set on having only Rod, and Kelli would have to find her own.

* * *

Three days later, tragedy struck: Rodney was missing.

"Daddy!" Gail came bursting into the kitchen, empty jar tenuously held in emotionally drained fingers. "Rodney is MISSING!"

"Oh, no!" Dad was visibly concerned, "What happened?"

Mom was at the table, as well. "When did you last see him?"

"Well," sobbed Gail, "Rod was tired, so we went to bed early. This morning, he was GONE!"

There was a bit of a pause. Mom and Dad looked at each other for a long moment. Then her dad responded, "Perhaps he got up early?" Gail nodded, willing to accept any explanation. Dad continued, "Yes. That's probably it. Was there food in the jar?"

Gail seemed surprised at the question. "Food?"

"Well, yeah. A guy's gotta eat, you know? Perhaps Ron went looking for something to munch on."

More tears were starting to gush, when mom interjected, "He meant Rod, Honey." Then turning to Dad with a stern glare that was somehow starkly impassive, "Daddy meant Rod."

"Of course," her dad continued, sheepish. "Rodney! I meant Rod." Fewer tears now. "Perhaps he was just hungry, and got lost on his way back from the... uh... garden?"

"So he's lost!!!" Gail was in full cry, at this point. "He's goooonnnne!"

"Hang on, Honey." Dad had his arm around Gail's shoulder by now. "I think I know how to get Rodney home."

"Hmff?" The question was slightly muffled, as Gail was wiping her nose on Dad's shirt.

"Well, I happen to know that fireflies love apples. Perhaps, if we were to put a bit of apple in the jar, your friend would find his way home!"

Mom jumped in again, saying, "Holes. We will need to fix the holes in the lid so he can't get out again."

Dad nodded. "Yes! Rodney obviously got out because the holes were too big. We'll replace the lid, too—with smaller holes in it."

Gail was satisfied with this plan. So much, so, in fact, that she immediately wriggled out of her dad's hug and ran to the counter, picking through the apples for the very ripest, tastiest looking apple she could find.

Part 2: Alec

Gail was bored. Just by looking at his daughter, Alec could tell that she was sad and frustrated. The troubling thing was, why? They were doing all the same fun stuff they always had done: trips to the river, new summer clothes, sleepovers with Kelli, family picnics, watching the off-season practices at the college field. None of it was working. The county fair was coming up in three days, but Gail just didn't seem excited about it. Not like last year, anyway. This summer was packed with all of the usual activities, yet Alec was watching his little girl mope about as though there was nothing at all to do.

Even now, from the kitchen window, Alec could see the slumped shoulders and bowed head, as her feet swung gently beneath the bench at the pond. The shawl he'd put in her basket lay next to her, along with the now empty jar and the cookie plate. Gail was singing softly to herself. Alec could almost hear the words, but not quite. He was sure she was making it up as she went, though. That would be just like her, using her creativity to keep herself occupied. Yet, somehow, Alec knew it wasn't enough.

Gail was flicking the flashlight off and on now. "What in the heck is she doing?" Alec thought. He smiled, and continued to watch, entranced at the inscrutable activities of his child. After some time, the singing stopped, and there was no light. The flashing beam skipped across the pond again for a minute or so. Then it stopped. Clearly, she was up to something. Was she trying to scare off a racoon, or perhaps a skunk? No, that wouldn't be it. Gail knew how to calmly move away from wild animals. His fatherly amusement grew as the cycle of flashing light and darkness continued.

He was wiping down the kitchen counter, and putting away the last remaining evidence of dinner, when Gail's raised voice commanded his attention. "Daddy! Daddy! Daddy!" She had abandoned everything at the bench and was running toward the house with the jar. "I've got a lightning bug! I got one, I GOT one!"

Alec met his daughter at the back door, a brief spike in adrenaline already fading as he saw she was okay. She held up the mason jar, which, in addition to traces of milk, contained the insect.

"I'm naming him 'Rodney'." Gail continued. "But we can call him 'Rod'," pausing, "Lightning Rod, get it?"

Alec had to stifle a snort as he laughed. Clever Gail! Of course, she would come up with a catchy name! He nodded his head merrily in agreement and said, "Yes, honey, I think that's a fine name! We need to poke some holes in the top, so it has some air, okay?"

Marche walked briskly through the kitchen door, slowing her pace as she saw the work that Alec and Gail were doing to fix up the jar. Her look turned to one of mild concern. "Abigail," she began, "are you sure you are ready to keep a pet? Do you know how to take care of a glow worm?"

Gail stopped what she was doing for a moment, heaved a dramatic sigh and said, "First, Rod is a lightning bug, not any kind of worm." She rolled her eyes emphatically and continued. "Also, he isn't a pet—he's my friend!" Indignant look, hands on her hips now. "And I think Rod and I can figure it out." She turned back to Alec. "I'm calling Kelli—can Kelli come over?"

There was nothing else for it. By the time Kelli showed up, Gail had Rodney's glass home enshrined atop her dresser, surrounded with decorations and a few flowers picked from the planter by the front door. Alec and Marche left the girls alone (or perhaps the girls deserted the adults – it's a matter of perspective.) Before bed, Marche asked, "Are you going to tuck Abigail in? You usually do, even when Kelli's here."

"I was debating that very question," Alec answered. "It kinda feels like I shouldn't. I don't know, it's like I've been replaced by a lampyrid."

"Perhaps you have!" Marche laughed, Alec joining in with only a slight delay.

Two days later, tragedy struck: Rodney was dead.

It was late at night. Alec was standing in the bedroom doorway. He held out the jar, now sporting a ribbon and several stickers, for Marche to examine. He said, "I'm going to replace him tonight, before she wakes up. I'm getting my shoes on and going out to catch another one right now."

Marche rolled her eyes, and said, "Oh my god, Alec!" She was simultaneously laughing and looking annoyed. "You can't protect her from her own mistakes! She decided she could handle this all on her own, and didn't want to talk it through. She didn't feed the thing, now it's dead. She's got to learn from that."

"Perhaps you're right," Alec was torn. "I mean, it's just a bug, after all. How sad could she get, really? She'll forget about it by the time we go to the fair on Saturday."

For a moment, Marche chuckled. But it was a dry laugh and she was more serious when she answered. "No, Alec. She won't. She'll be very sad, and probably for a while. She'll feel a twang of guilt every time she sees a mason jar, and that will certainly last for weeks. Maybe longer. She'll probably want to get him a Christmas card and mail it to heaven." She added with another dry chuckle.

"So... I'm confused. You make it sound bad." He paused. Marche said nothing, so he went on. "I know she'll be really bummed out. I can fix this. I'm going out to the pond!"

"Alec," Marche sighed deeply, "you can't always fix things for Abigail." She shifted to a lighter tone. "Yes, she's very attached to that stupid bug. It's hard to explain, but you need to let her go through this."

"You mean the grieving process." It was a statement.

"No. Well, yes." She slowed down a bit, picking her words. "Your daughter is shedding her tiny childhood feelings and starting to experience big ones. Like losing your baby teeth ...it takes time."

Alec was silent.

"She needs to learn how to chew on her adult emotions. You can't take that from her."

Alec had been sitting on the corner of the bed, examining the jar. After a few moments of reflection, he came up with a compromise. "Fine, then." he said, standing. "Rodney escaped." With that, he unscrewed the lid, dumped the dead bug into the wastebasket, and went to put the jar back in Gail's room.

The next morning, Marche and Alec were silently drinking coffee. There was an unspoken question waiting patiently with them, like an invisible cat coiling its legs to pounce. Alec knew Marche was right. Marche was certain Alec could not maintain the charade; both of them wondered how Alec's little "escaped bug" ruse would work out. The little bird entered the room and scared the cat away.

"Daddy!" Gail came bursting into the kitchen, empty jar tenuously held in her limp, emotionally drained fingers, "Rodney is MISSING!"

There were looks back and forth. For a fleeting second, Marche thought about responding with something like, "I'm sorry, Honey. Here, have some toast and jam." Or maybe adopt a sardonic attitude and say, "Oh, wow! Perhaps you should have been more thorough in locking up your victim!" But she refrained, and she waited, with her eye on Alec and his suddenly pale complexion.

"Oh, no!" Alec was visibly concerned, "What happened?"

Marche played along. "When did you last see him?" she asked.

"Well," Gail was sobbing now. Alec reached out to take the jar, thinking the girl would drop it. But she clung to it and continued. "Rod was tired, so we went to bed early. This morning, he was GONE!"

There was a pause. Marche and Alec had talked about this. The plan was to offer comfort and move on as quickly as possible. However, Alec ventured a hypothesis. "Perhaps he got up early?" Gail nodded. She was clearly brightening up with this idea, so Alec continued, "Yes. That's probably it. Was there food in the jar?"

Gail seemed surprised at the question. "Food?"

Marche could almost feel the moment when Alec's resolve came crashing down. She watched as Alec unfolded a plan to set out some food, and she knew, without a doubt, that Rodney would indeed return that night.

Epilogue

Sure enough, the next day, Rodney was back. Gail never asked him where he had been, or what he had been doing. It's not that she didn't care, either. Gail felt that, deep down, she already knew the answer. It turned out that Rodney actually did like bits of freshly cut apple, and he fared quite well for some time. A couple of nights later, Kelli caught a firefly, too. His name turned out to be "Sparky," and he never wandered off.

After a few weeks, Gail and Kelli decided that their tiny friends would probably be happier back at the pond, with all of the other lightning bugs—Sparky and Rodney's own friends and family. As the summer had worn on, there were noticeably fewer lights among the reeds and over the water. It was definitely time. So in a late August twilight, there stood Mom, Dad, Gail, Kelli and about a dozen toy bears, dogs, and unicorns. All were gathered around the bench by the pond to open the jars and release the lightning bugs. Gail hushed them all and paused for a few words.

"Rodney," she said, "the once lost lightning bug, and Sparky, the brightest firefly we've ever known." She stopped, reaching down into the basket for a paper plate. It had writing on it, and it was taped to what looked like a single chopstick, probably pilfered from a kitchen drawer. Gail and Kelli walked the few steps to the edge of the water, and together they ceremoniously stuck it in the ground, like a small signpost.

Gail started her little speech over from the beginning. "Rodney," she said, "the lost lightning bug, who returned to us, and Sparky, the brightest firefly we've ever known." She paused for effect, "we now mem… memory…"

"Memorialize…?" said Dad.

"Yes. That. We memorialize your names with the declaration that this will be known as the 'Lightning Rod and Sparky Pond,' to forever remind us of our most enjoyable friendship this summer!" The two girls opened the jars. The fireflies flew out and, as far as Alec could tell, turned to wave goodbye before buzzing off over the swampy shore.

The deed was done. The girls gathered their stuffed animals. Everyone headed back to the house.

"So, you know school starts Monday, right?" asked Alec as they walked.

"Yeah," said Gail. "When is that, exactly?"

"That's three days."

"Wow!" said Gail. "Summer went by so fast!"

Candy, Bags, and Purity

Sasha sat on the bench with her back to the street, waiting for the bus. Her knees ached from one final adolescent growth spurt, her feet were sore after walking the long miles from the farm, and her heart felt heavy with the weight of dark fears and winter nights. Now that she was in the city, she was conflicted. On one hand, opportunities were peeking from around each building, like the glinting eyes of nighttime critters. They were looking for breadcrumbs and nuts from her hand, waiting for her move. Opportunities for change, for a future, for a different life. Yet there was also the black stain.

It had started in the middle of her chest, but it was growing. It was spreading, covering her core like the soot of a thousand coal chambers. It was a dark shadow that refused the light, even the sunlight. Creeping out onto her arms, the darkness carried with it a cold touch, prickly with sharp quills. To her legs, it was the stickers of frozen star thistle, piercing her as she forged through a lonely hibernal solstice. It was sticky on her hands, like the tar found on the roads or the grease of the train tracks, and it would never, ever wash off. Sasha could not name the fear, but somewhere inside she felt it would ruin everything, that it would engulf everything, weighing her down like inescapable gravity.

Slumping on the bench with her few belongings stacked in her lap, she looked at her reflection in the shop window, at her face, her hands, her forearms. No, the black stain could not be seen with the eye, but Sasha knew it was there. She could feel it. She noticed a sign painted in the window, at which she had stared for several minutes before seeing it. Even then it was not the words but the logo that caught her attention. The image was the silhouette of a young woman, perhaps only a girl, with a small suitcase in one hand, and holding a lollipop in the other. The name of the store was "Candy, Bags, and Purity." "Huh," she thought to herself, then decided to check it out. She gathered up her armful of things and went to the entrance.

An ancient metal hand bell rang out loudly as she walked inside, its springy bracket reacting violently to the motion of the door. When the door closed, the bell rang again, and when it did the noise of the city street was suddenly silenced. Well, nearly so. There were still the low rumblings of motors, especially trucks, but the busy buzz of downtown life was gone. The late afternoon sun sloped through the air, highlighting a few motes of airborne dust that surfed the eddies and flows created by Sasha's intrusion. She hesitated, hovering near the door, waiting to get a look at the proprietor. She was surprised that nobody was there to greet her, after the loud clanging of the door.

From where she stood, Sasha examined the room. There were rows of apple baskets scattered around the front half, which was lined with glass-fronted cabinets. The baskets were full of individual candies, mix-and-match, pay by the pound. The cases on the left contained rows and rows of colorful boxes, in which Sasha could make out off-season candy canes, shortbread biscuits, candied raisins, and spice drops. The case on the right held chocolates in neat, narrow trays, with handwritten names and descriptions posted on tiny placards along the front.

The back half of the room was completely full of luggage. Suitcase sets were de-nested and stacked to make tall narrow pyramids, like a maze of square towers planted all over the floor. On the walls hung an astonishing variety of duffels, totes, knapsacks, waist packs, messenger bags, gym bags, bags for parents to carry baby things. There were briefcases and valet rolls, garment bags and laptop covers. If you needed to take it with you, this store seemed to have something to pack it in.

She waited a moment (that seemed like several long minutes) then called out, "Hello?"

Almost immediately, as if on cue, a woman sauntered casually from the back room. "Hello there!" The woman was not tall, and not thin. She was not, by any measure, young, but she was not frail. Most importantly, however, she did not seem threatening. Sasha began to relax, taking another step away from the door, further into the shop. The woman continued. "I'm Mary." Then, with a sweeping gesture, "If you need anything, just ask!" Her smile seemed involuntary, as if she just couldn't help being happy, right here in this room, right now, doing exactly this. Sasha smiled weakly but made no remark.

Mary went about organizing some things behind the counter. Clinking of glass jars, sliding sounds, and the soft rush of terry cloth as she dusted an empty space on the shelf. Sasha looked around the room, afraid to ask for help. She began to walk slowly in a wide arc away from the counter. Finally, without looking at Mary, she remarked, "This shop has a funny name." She said it in a flat tone, as if she were alone, her words having been intended only for the bits of dust in the air, no one else.

Mary's casual laugh had the familiar "ho-ho-ho" sound of a storybook Santa Claus, but sweet, and earthy, as though she'd cultivated it on a farm somewhere before bringing it with her to the city. "I sell candy, and suitcases. What else would you call it?"

"Do you sell 'purity,' too?" Sasha gestured around, "I don't see any on the shelves…"

Mary laughed again, but it ended in a sigh this time. Her tone changed, somewhat wistful now. "People come and go, looking for all sorts of things." She turned her head slightly to the right, looking past Sasha to an empty space at the end of the counter. Mary continued looking in that direction as she said, "Most don't even know what they're looking for in the first place."

Sasha followed the woman's gaze and saw that the space was not actually empty: there was a single chair, low and small, just beyond the last cabinet. The chair looked like an antique, and seemed like it should have a doll or teddy bear sitting in it for display. But the chair was bare, and Mary had probably only stared into random space as she spoke, as people sometimes do.

But Sasha couldn't resist the bait of this enigmatic statement. "What exactly does 'purity' even mean?"

Mary sat down on a barstool by the register. "Well, I suppose it's a lot of things." Pause. "Wholesomeness, cleanliness, virtue, decency, for starters. It can also refer to clarity, or concentration. The world's religions all talk about 'purity,' with meanings that range from innocence and chastity to integrity and altruism." Another pause. "People have been known to come here looking for one or more of those things, or even all of them at once."

Sasha remained silent. Inside, she could feel herself rolling her eyes, but she was possessed of her expressions well enough to simply look skeptical. Mary continued.

"But you didn't come in here for anything so abstract, did you? You came in looking for candy, I'm sure of it. A kid in a candy store, as they say, no doubt about it!" Again, Mary laughed aloud, a tone that radiated out from her place at the counter in light, infectious peals.

"Actually," Sasha said, "I need a suitcase. A small one, like that." She pointed across the shop, to the back wall.

Somehow, Mary seemed as though she was expecting this. "Ah yes," she said, "the carpet bags are popular right now." She was already nearing the display, and pointed, "This one, perhaps?"

Sasha nodded, then added, "Yes. That's exactly the one I noticed when I first came in."

"It's a good bag." Mary carried it slowly, in what was apparently her characteristic saunter, back to the front of the store, chatting in a contemplative tone. "Funny thing," she was saying, "but we say 'carpetbagger' to describe an outsider who is trying to blend in. Usually, one who's trying to take advantage." Then she placed the bag into Sasha's hands and stepped back behind the counter.

"Oh?" Sasha wondered if there was some point to this line of prattle.

"Yeah. But I don't know. Sometimes outsiders aren't outsiders at all. We don't know where they come from, or why they left there. Many are probably just insiders who don't happen to feel like they belong. It's just a matter of intention. If your motives are pure, then…" She trailed off and looked up.

Inside, Sasha was rolling her imaginary eyes again, but managed a smile.

Mary looked down at the object in Sasha's hands, as if just noticing it. "A good bag. Not very big, but roomy inside. Comes with a free sucker," she added, with an upbeat tone.

Sasha thought immediately of the shop logo she'd noticed outside. She smiled, and said, "I'll look just like the girl on your sign!" and then started to laugh. It was a derisive and rather hoarse sound, and strange to her ears. It was like the caw of a crow that faded to the yapping of excited dogs in the distance. The girl's rusty laugh brought a slow, silent smile to Mary's face. She chuckled, reached out her hand, and dropped a piece of candy into the bag with a nod.

At this point Sasha found herself looking again at the empty chair, in the empty corner. It seemed positioned just so. Intentionally, strategically placed. There was something odd about it that said, "Reserved," or something like that. It seemed clear that you were not supposed to sit there. She looked back at Mary, who was watching the girl's face closely.

"That's my daughter's chair," she said. There was an uncharacteristic, low tone to Mary's voice. "Purity died tragically when she was fourteen. I can still see her in that chair, so I keep her with me in the shop."

There followed several moments of silence. The seconds hung like dark birds, materializing one at a time until twenty or thirty were gliding in the warm rising air of some desert canyon's ochre rim. Somewhere, a clock was probably ticking, but not here. Eventually, Sasha took a slow, deep breath, exhaled, and said, "I know exactly what that feels like." Mary looked to the chair, then back at the girl in front of her, nodding once with no comment.

Sasha paid for her bag, said her goodbyes, and walked out of the shop. The bell overhead jingled as she opened the door. Then, when it rang again, the sound of the city street resumed, making the young woman wonder how long she'd been in the store. It seemed like hours but was probably only a few minutes. She stepped over to the bench and sat down facing the street. She didn't look back, but she imagined that Mary was likely humming a song to herself, as she dusted and cleaned and organized.

But Mary stood by the register, watching through the window. She spoke out loud. "I wish I could go with her, to look out for her."

"You know she connected with me, right?" This voice came from the end of the counter. "She could feel me sitting here."

"I know."

Purity paused, then said softly, "She has the black stain. I can see it."

Mary didn't turn away from the window. "I'm so sorry I didn't see what was happening to you until it was too late."

"You're the best mother I could have ever had, in this life or the last." Purity remained, as always, in the chair, but still seemed to convey the impression of a hug in her voice.

"Thank you, Purity."

"She'll be okay, I can tell. She's not going back. Ever."

"You have inside information?"

"Not this time." Purity gave a little giggle. "Just a gut feeling."

"I'll trust that, then."

Outside, Sasha was boarding the bus. Her head was high, shoulders thrown back, and she carried the seeds of her new life in a single carpet bag. She looked back once, to see only her own reflection in the windows of the shop. Then the shop started to slide to the right. The whole block went by, and eventually the rest of the city scrolled past her window, until there was nothing but rolling hills dotted with flowers under a setting sun. Sasha tucked her knees up to her chest, leaned against the wall, and prepared herself to wake up in a different world.

The Apothecary

Karly stood before the large, storefront window of the apothecary shop for a long minute. She was admiring, once again, the scarves decorating the various objects of the display. It was March, and the seasonal exhibit now rang out in the diverse colors of impending spring blooms. There were apple crate shelves supporting bottles of liquid in rose pink and butterscotch gold, alongside baskets of decorative soaps in violet, teal, and candy red. An aged wicker chair supported a carefully disorganized stack of lady's hats, collected from vintage memories of magnificent theatre, riverboat rides, far away cities and trips to the zoo.

The center of the display was an animal marionette, in the form of a large, spotted dog. It was a dalmatian, Karly decided, made from painted wood, with leather for its joints and ears. The dog-puppet was suspended from the ceiling, the strings holding it in midflight as it jumped over a pickling crock of dried hydrangeas: a brilliant and colorful obstacle for the starkly beautiful black and white dog. The backdrop of the whole thing was a parchment dressing screen on which were hung several colorful hand fans. Some of these were fully open to show bright painted scenes from folklore and song, others partially folded, their stories collapsing in corrugated abstraction.

But Karly admired the scarves. Not because of their prominence, as they were simply draped about and under the other things which made up the giant diorama. Karly felt that she had seen nothing in her entire twelve years as beautiful as these simple bolts of cloth. They flowed in a random, liquid form over and engulfing the half-concealed objects beneath, a coy game of peekaboo between art and physics, lazy cats melting into the potted plants of a sunny window box.

There were perhaps a dozen scarves in the window. Several were of a light blue, spread about like the reflection of the sky in placid waters, cool and sweet. A few of them were dyed in broad stripes of yellow—warm, lemony bands flanking a single strip of white, undyed cotton. There were three in different shades of orange, colors which Karly decided to name "freshly pulled carrot," "washed carrot," and "peeled carrot," as they ranged from darker to lighter in shade.

Then there was the red one. It was the only one she didn't like, and the girl wondered why it was even included in the display. It was at once the color of blood, rage, and violence. It looked like the coals of resentment that glowed beneath a kettle of hate, like the burning eyes of some ancient demon, crouching to strike the innocent passersby from its dark, awful recess.

Karly tried to see the lighter side, scouring her memories for images of happy things in that hue. Roses, symbols of love, in deep, wine red. But, no, they have thorns. Mustn't forget those awful things. The warmth and safety of a bright red campfire is nice. However, once escaped, the same fire would engulf an entire forest, along with any house which might inadvertently wander into the fire's infernal path. The beautiful berries of the holly bush, of course, which used to deck the halls at Christmas. Why didn't we have them anymore? Oh, yes, Karly recalled: she had eaten a few of them when she was five or six and gotten so sick the doctor was called to treat the poison. She gave up trying to rationalize the choice of window dressing and turned her steps inside.

The apothecary sat on a tall stool behind the counter, drinking from a slender cup while he read the morning paper. Karly stopped abruptly at the sight of him. All describable features faded to gray leaving only a crimson swath: he was wearing one of the red scarves draped loosely about his neck. She felt her face flush slightly, as though an odd breeze somehow both hot and cold, had brushed her cheek, and the quiet metronome in her chest sped up a bit in response.

"Hellooo, there!" The baritone voice had a lilt to it, which lent a disarming lightness in spite of its depth (and the apothecary's girth.) "What can I do for you today?"

Karly's heart began to slow a bit, a palpable echo of hospitality ringing after the man's words. She felt unexpectedly safe, realizing she had quickly judged the apothecary by nothing more than a scrap of colored cloth, and blushed again. She quickly gathered her wits and recalled her mission.

"I need tea, please." Pause. "Tea for an upset stomach."

"Oooh," he nodded, "I have just the thing." He reached behind him, without looking, and opened a drawer. His hand dipped inside briefly, then knuckled the drawer closed in a single, smooth motion, swinging around to deposit a small packet on the counter. "Ginger," he declared, "is the mother of all herbs." He chuckled, saying, "This is my own blend. Drink it hot or cold."

Karly was peering down the row of drawers now, floor to ceiling, filling two full walls of the shop. "You have so many of them," she asked, "how do you keep track?"

A deep laugh rolled from the apothecary's chest, "Well, you know… I've been at this a while. I don't recall everything here all the time, but I always seem to find things when I need them."

The drawers, although ranked by size, were of various colors. Some had labels, others not. Some fit neatly into their designated sockets, while others were more like rows of similar boxes on shelves. With mismatched handles and knobs, the whole array made a kind of random mosaic, discordant but somehow euphonious at the same time, like the colorful flow of crowds at an open-air market, blended together in the early light of a summer morning.

"What's in that one?" Karly pointed at a greenish drawer with a yellow knob.

The apothecary turned in his seat to look. "Happiness." He said simply.

"Really? You have a drawer of happiness?"

"Oh, I have many kinds of happiness here." The apothecary gave a bouncy nod. "There are over a thousand drawers in this shop, most of which are divided into several additional boxes inside. Then there are the jars, pots, and crocks on the other wall. In the back room, there are bags and pallets containing ingredients for more things than even I can imagine. And I can imagine a great many things. Many of these are, indeed, some form of happiness."

Karly now had her elbows on the counter, hands under her chin in rapt attention. "Like what?" she asked, "What else do you have in here?"

"What do you need?" He shrugged, and continued without waiting for an answer, "I have treatments for all of the common ailments: cold and flu, fevers and chills. I have an elixir for arthritis and another for aching backs. I have something for the pain one gets in her head from worrying too much, and the same thing can be used to treat menstrual cramps." He was pointing, as he talked, at drawers in the immediate vicinity of the chair. Now he stood and began to move slowly down the long counter. "I have chamomile and valerian, if you are anxious or cannot rest. I have echinacea, gingko, milk thistle, Saint John's wort, to treat everything from asthma to gout to problems of the liver. I have ginseng." He paused. "You know what that's for?" Karly shook her head. "Everything!" he said, laughing. "All of these ingredients have a variety of uses, and ginseng has the most!"

As he walked, Karly had followed slowly down the long counter, occasionally looking up at the apothecary, but mostly at the countertop, where she had been tracing the grain of the wood with her finger. She almost bumped into him when he stepped through the open flap of the bar gate, out into the room. She looked up, but he was now turning to point in various directions.

"I have potions, ointments, and elixirs for doctors, too. Treatments for colicky babies, and elderly digestion. I have cream for severe burns, powders to stop bleeding, and strong drinks to prepare a patient for surgery. These things make the world a better place, don't you think?" Karly made noises of agreement into a non-existent pause. "But the usefulness of other things can be hard to see at times—at least to see them in their fullest extent."

Karly was getting curious again, a fact which must have shown on her face. The apothecary continued, sounding somewhat like a carnival barker extolling the virtues of his marvelous wares.

"I have a drawer over there that has keys to various interesting things, and another that has only buttons. Somewhere in that corner is a cure for cancer, although I haven't actually assembled it yet. There are drawers of summer sunshine, autumn leaves, and candied peel for winter's baking. In this room are the tears of a parent, and alongside them is the first homerun of the season. The jars hold clean bandages, romantic connections, found socks, future generations of holiday gatherings, and empty space for the thoughts of our elders. Somewhere in this shop are unwritten novels, repaired cartwheels, rodeo rides, bridges to faraway shores, warm regards, the rise and fall of governments—each of them waiting to be placed in the hands of the right person."

Although Karly was somewhat dazzled with the wonder of it all, she had a nagging question. She asked, "Can we go back to the happiness?"

"Ah. You are interested in that, are you? So, what do you think might be in that drawer?" The apothecary began moving back to his original position behind the counter, eventually to sit in his ancient, spindly chair with a slight squeak.

Karly thought it over. "I don't know. Something that makes me happy, I guess...?"

"And what makes you happy, Karleen?"

"Warm things?" It was a questioning sort of answer. "I think happy, warm things."

The apothecary turned and reached, removing the whole box, and set it on the counter in front of the girl. "Lucky you." He said simply.

Before Karly even looked into the drawer, she could smell its contents. She perked up visibly. "That smells goooood!"

It was like opening a pie cupboard in late December, with the warm, spicy steam of mincemeat spilling out and caressing your face. The smell was that of a magical, foreign land, whose roads were paved with cardamom shells and cinnamon bark was used as writing paper. The smell was the texture and color of her grandfather's tweed jacket, seen every Friday when he would take Grandma dancing at the speakeasy on 57th Street. It was like hot apple cider, served with rum cake.

Karly was somewhat disappointed when she looked at the actual contents of the box, which had three compartments of dry, brown, crumbly stuff.

"What is it?"

"Cinnamon, clove, and garam masala." He was beginning to scoop a little of each into a small muslin bag.

"This is 'happiness'?" She seemed skeptical.

"Is it not? You seemed to like the smell. Wait until you taste it." He smiled, rising and walked a short distance down the bar. He lit a burner under a large water kettle and returned. He explained, "We make a pot of tea, and add a teaspoon of this mix to it. We will let it steep for a while, then add honey and cream. It's known as 'chai'."

While the apothecary set about the rest of the tea preparations, Karly asked a new question. "Why are there so many colors on the drawers? And the knobs have been painted too. Why?"

The apothecary looked up and down the row before answering, as though refreshing his memory regarding the look of the shop. He explained. "The drawers have gotten moved around over the years, for convenience. At one time, all of the drawers of a single color would have been grouped together. There was a brown cabinet, a green cabinet, a lavender cabinet, and the several natural wood colors, of course. Because I get into some drawers much more frequently than others, I've moved those closer to my stool, for easy reach."

Karly giggled. "I thought it meant something!"

The apothecary gave one of his deep, resonant laughs. "Well," he continued. "Mostly not. A few of the drawers have been painted for other reasons. The knobs are another story. The handle on each drawer is color coded to indicate who is allowed to open that drawer." Karly's mind was racing, her eyes scanning the drawers, as he continued. "The blue knobs, and there are only a few, are available to anyone who is aware of them; anyone who is given any access can use the contents of those drawers." Karly listened intently, spotting the blue knobs scattered about. "The orange knobs are for the fully trained alchemist, and only they should be granted access to such important things."

Karly suddenly made a connection, but held back, asking only, "The knobs painted yellow with the white strip—who opens those?"

"Ah! Those are for students. Anyone who has chosen to study under the apothecary, and who has been accepted, is free to peruse the daffodil handles, as we call them."

"These colors are the same as the scarves in the window!"

"Correct." The apothecary raised an eyebrow but made no remark as he poured the water from the kettle into the teapot.

"I love the scarves. They're beautiful. Well, mostly." She paused, but then continued in childish disregard of tact. "I don't like the red one."

The apothecary let out a robust laugh this time, and asked, "They're technically pashmina, by the way. But...why not? You don't like red?"

Karly's brows knit, and she said, "Well, it's a scary color. Anger, blood, fire are all scary things. I can't think of anything red that is not at least partly bad. Like, the way red roses have vicious thorns! Red means danger, don't you see?"

The apothecary nodded, thoughtful for a moment. "What about strawberries, then? I don't believe those are dangerous." He smiled before continuing, "You are, in part, correct." He spoke in a low voice now, in a conspiratorial tone, as though he was about to give secret information. "Red is a very powerful color, with—it's true—with elements good and bad. The saffron-red pashmina is granted to the alchemist of the highest level. It is red, in part, because it is so easily seen, although that's true of the orange pashmina as well. In the great scheme of things, red is the deepest color, the root, if you will, of all colors. The slowest vibration of which all other vibrations are harmonics. It is the outermost color of the rainbow, and the last color of the fading sunset." Karly was rapidly losing interest in the metaphysical lecture and had begun searching for any drawers with red knobs.

She only found one. "What's in that drawer?" She pointed. "The black drawer, with the red knob?"

In his usual habit of deliberation, the apothecary looked at the drawer, the only black drawer, at the far bottom corner of the wall behind the counter. He didn't respond right away.

Karly continued, asking, "And why is it the only black one?" She was getting more curious by the moment. "Is the cabinet it came from gone?"

"No," A slow sigh, then, "That one seems to have darkened of its own accord. The black drawer is for any and all things that are foul in nature. Evil things." He gave the tea a stir and put the lid back on.

"Well," Karly had only the vaguest of notions of what might be meant by "evil," but nothing she could think of would fit in that small box. "What's in it?"

The apothecary didn't answer. He got up from his chair, walked casually down the length of the counter, and retrieved the drawer. He set it wordlessly between them.

The presence, up close, of the evil drawer was more than a little disconcerting, and Karly was regretting her curiosity. She held her gaze high and kept it there while a lump in her throat rose, then slowly receded again. She felt a wave of dread, fear, anger. Then a pang of inexplicable guilt, and a resignation to follow through with her original inquiry. She looked into the drawer.

"It's empty!" She said, both relieved and confused.

The apothecary looked into the drawer, tipping it slightly to see every corner. "So it is."

Karly stared blankly back.

"You see, Karleen, this is no ordinary drawer." He pushed it slightly to one side, but only enough to make a clear space in which to pour the tea. "In this particular box," he nodded his head slightly, "things come and go. We can put things in it, but we have no guarantee that they'll still be there when we look again." He poured two cups of the chai, adding cream and sugar as he spoke. "This is why only I can open the drawer. We never know what we may or may not find."

"But why?" Karly was perplexed. "You said it was for everything evil. Why have such a drawer? Why keep it?" Then she took her first sip of chai, and abruptly exclaimed, "Oh my god!" looking at the cup in her hands. "This stuff is amazing! What's it called again? I need to know what to ask for!"

He answered, and the two laughed for several moments. Eventually, the apothecary addressed the question.

"Why keep the black box, you wonder? This is hard to explain. Sometimes we need exactly such a place. I think it's easier if I just show you."

The apothecary produced a small notepad from somewhere behind the counter and slid it across to Karly. Then he handed her a pen.

"What is your worst fear? Your darkest memory? You have something. We all do. Something you would never tell anyone." He paused, waiting as Karly thought for a few moments. When she looked back to his face, the apothecary said, "Okay. You don't need to write it all down, but I want you to put a word on the paper. Or draw something. Or just put some mark, anything at all on the paper, and you will find that it will become attached to this dark thing that you carry."

Karly had come up blank, with nothing specific to write. She felt that she wanted to do this, however. It was as though she had some compelling reason for it, a reason that was just a teeny bit out of reach at the moment, a fuzzy shadow in a low corner nearby. Her hand moved quickly on the notepad, leaving a squiggle that she knew, somehow, would mean something to her later.

"Now put that in the box."

She dropped it in as instructed. The little note fell slowly, tipping back and forth not unlike the motion of a falling feather. It fell for a long time, slower and slower, getting smaller in the distance. Now it was just a tiny, white dab on an inky black backdrop of empty space inside the drawer of evil. Eventually, it hit the bottom with a loud "clang," like the locks of a heavy prison door banging together in the still silence of some remote, timeless night.

"Thank you," said the apothecary. "You will know when it's time to come back and look into that drawer.

She said nothing, sipping her chai in silence, feet swinging below her as she sat, waiting for the apothecary to speak again.

But he did not. Instead, he stood, and returned to the end of the counter, replacing the drawer in its slot. He came out from behind the counter, and walked up to the window display, reaching around the dressing screen. After a bit of rustling about, he pushed the screen back into its proper place and then returned to his stool. In his hand he held one of the blue scarves, which he proceeded to fold carefully on the bar.

Then he pushed it over to Karly, saying, "You'll know when it's time to open that drawer, Karleen. Save this, and show it when you come in."

* * *

Karleen woke up, the long-forgotten memory of a black apothecary box—with a red handle—suddenly vivid in her mind. She got out of bed, brushed her teeth, and made her way downstairs to the kitchen. She ate a light breakfast, then moved out to the garden to sip her tea and continue the process of waking up, slowly merging her reality with the larger world around her.

The house was too quiet these days. With her youngest in college, and the rest of the family estranged or gone, Karleen felt simultaneously free of her daily obligations and imprisoned by her inner shadows. And for some reason, today, she was thinking about an apothecary, a black drawer, and a note that she couldn't quite recall.

Was it a dream? Or was she remembering something that actually happened to her twelve-year-old self? She had so few memories from that time, and even fewer from her life before that. She had lived with her grandparents then, she knew that much, although she was unable to recall why. It was a peaceful time, she thought, even if she couldn't quite remember why that was so. Curiosity won out, and she decided to start her weekend by looking through a few of her old boxes, long stored in the deep recesses of the closet under the stairs.

She dragged the first box out into the middle of the living room floor. It held nothing but sheet music from the bench and shelves at Grandma's piano. That was it. Pages upon pages of chords and notes, like so many ants that crawled across endless sheets of staff-paper. She stacked them carefully and dumped them back in the box.

The second was full to the brim with toys, scrapbooks, photos, documents, awards, schoolwork, and an embroidered pillowcase, all of which had been packed by Grandma at the end of middle school. Karleen paused for a few moments to admire one of the photographs. It was Juniper, the exuberant dalmatian of her early childhood, now subdued in a framed print. Then she replaced the contents of that box and moved on.

In the third one, she discovered Grandpa's collection of hand-painted lead toys. It was a very heavy package, made somewhat lighter by the presence of several cigar boxes in the bottom. These, in turn, held greeting cards from roughly a decade of birthdays and Christmases, which gave Karleen a spark of hope: she had packed this box herself, after Grandpa had passed away.

Sure enough, she struck gold in the next one. In it was Missy, her favorite doll, and a tiny, doll-sized blanket. There were candles, which she had kept hidden as a girl since she would be in big trouble if she were ever caught with fire. There were small collections of shells, stones, and a few interesting coins of little collector's value. But most of all, and a huge surprise, was the blue scarf.

She held it up to the sunlight streaming through the living room windows, seeing how the old fabric filtered the bright rays into so many pinholes. She felt the fabric. Was it cotton? Or a very soft wool? Even after more than three decades of storage, the color was a striking, vibrant blue, the reflection of the sky in placid waters, or the deep cracks in a glacier of ancient ice. Holding it up to her face, she could feel the soft presence of distant hands, working the cloth with care, fashioning it into this ... what was it called? A pashmina, wasn't it? And there was a smell, under the veil of musty closet, and time and dust—a warm, glowing smell: the scent of happiness.

Karleen began to cry. She didn't feel silly about it, or self-conscious. (There was nobody at home, anyway.) She knew that this meant something, and she felt memories sparkling like fireflies under a table of imaginary glass. She felt the memories, not as ones connected to the scarf itself, but deeper, and she knew also that the scarf was the key.

It was time. Karleen gathered the scarf, her shoes, and her wits, and moments later was out the door. She was filled with hope that she might find the black apothecary box, and dread that she might find something waiting inside.

Not Going Back

Carrie sat under the willow tree, considering the diminishing sunset and the rapidly advancing night. Her left hand rested on the stone bench, which had been warming slowly under her touch. "If I move my hand…" she spoke to the tree, the fireflies, the overseer's house beyond the pond, "If I were to move it right now, it would be cold under my palm." She repositioned as she spoke. "It would be cold for some time," she looked up, into the weeping branches, a living umbrella, shielding her from the dew that would eventually come if she remained outside, "perhaps a long time. But then it would become warm again, because of my touch." With this she raised her hand, turning it toward her, then away, examining it like a freshly picked flower. "I'm leaving," she told it.

The house was empty for the weekend, nobody would return for two days. From the second story window, Carrie could see the distant skyline of New Orleans, irregular boxes in sunrise silhouette. She could imagine iron railings on rows of townhouses, lining cobblestone streets awash in fog, bourbon and soot rain. There was no place for her there. It was too far from her heart, and too close to home. She looked down, into the courtyard. Even now, the square cut flagstones were inviting, calling her, promising a nice, soft landing. "It would be so, so easy," she shook her head. The siren song of the jump, however, was barely audible over the voice of the steamer trunk. "Remember," it was saying in a deep baritone, incongruently like the voice of Santa Claus, "Remember, we're leaving."

It lay there, open, exposing the invisible future that would remain once this day was gone. Packing was simultaneously a depressing slog and an adrenaline-charged leap. It was a long series of decisions, large and small, but different than she had anticipated. In a way, the trunk had started out full—overflowing, in fact. All the bits and pieces of hearth and home vying for a seat on this, the last departing ship. This was a day spent looking around the room, the house, the worldly circle, and saying, "Not this," and "not that." Eventually, the trunk was ready to go. It was full of those things which were left once Carrie had removed from the pile everything she would not need. Much like extracting the teeth that were causing the pain, that were threatening to abscess.

Carrie could not lift the trunk. So, she dragged it. Bumping down the stairs, leaving deep scratches in the hardwood floor of the entry hall, grinding across the brickwork to the carriage house. By the time she had tilted, flipped, and levered the single piece of luggage into a cart, her dress was torn, soiled, and damp with sweat the length of her back. Carrie was a mess. While she went about selecting a driving harness (and retrieving the finest horse in the stable), Carrie's mind kept wandering back to the house where there could be a bath and clean clothes. "No." She spoke to the horse, cinching the last strap. "Not going back."

At the train station in New Orleans, there was the slow bustle of late afternoon weekday business, with a fair number of passengers and quite a bit of freight arriving and departing Louisiana's biggest terminal. A pair of couriers were astonished, but very happy to accept the horse and cart in exchange for baggage handling. They followed Carrie into the station with the trunk. One of the men stayed with her until she had finished purchasing her ticket, then moved the trunk to the loading ramp for her. He lingered for a moment, as Carrie surveyed the boarding area, looking for her platform number.

"One way?" He had seen her making the purchase, so he was making an observation, not really a question. The woman's eyes flashed a bit with anger, or perhaps fear, as she looked at him. She wondered why he was still standing there, but said nothing.

"Listen," the courier said, "That's a real nice horse you gave us. And a well-made cart—better than ours." He paused, searching her face for a moment. "Anyway, it don't seem fair to just take it, even if you did offer it." He was reaching in his pockets now, pulling out a handful of coins and a few crumpled bills. He didn't count it, he simply reached out, grabbing her hand, and shoved the money in it, closing her fingers around it for her. Carrie had to clap her free hand over it to keep from dropping some. "There," he declared. "We're even now." He released her hand, smiled, and turned away.

Carrie looked at the sum she held. It was a significant amount, probably more than doubling her carefully saved reserves. Perhaps it wasn't the full value of the horse and cart, it was hard to say for sure, but it was apparently all the man had. She was shocked, uncertain how to feel. Standing there on the platform, Carrie sighed deeply. It was the relief that comes at the end of the line, just like the very building around her. But the Southern Railway Terminal was also a beginning, and in this new, strange adventure, Carrie suddenly felt she was less alone than she had been for years. She suddenly realized that she hadn't thanked the courier, quickly scanning the area in her sight. But he was gone, and her train had arrived.

It was a long ride. The rickety emigrant-class car was decades out of date, but the ticket was cheap. There was no food service in this car, and no place to sleep. Unlike the pullman passengers, people in these seats were expected to bring their own food and, if sleep was necessary, it would either be upright or leaning against each other on the wooden benches. Carrie had some dried pork in her pocket, hastily wrapped in parchment on her way out the door. And there was water aboard the train. These would be her sustenance for the next seven days.

Several passengers left the car in Houston late the next day. Carrie had not yet slept, sitting silently as the sunrise behind them drew long shadows on the swampy south, then erasing them slowly through noon, only to redraw the dark outlines again in the afternoon hours. The bench was now empty, and the train had begun its rhythmic, soporific motion again. Next stop would be a few hours out, and the terminal was still most of a week away. After eating a few bites, Carrie lay down and slept the slow, hollow sleep of the dead.

Eventually, she started to dream. She dreamed she was in the San Antonio station, brightly lit, but quiet in the late-night hour. But it was also El Paso, and the smell of diesel was replacing the dense air of the gulf region. Inside, she could feel the train stop, pause, and restart, and imagined an elevator door opening to release the pent-up souls traveling to the top floor. She opened her eyes briefly in Tucson, surprised to find cushions on the benches, and an announcer calling for passengers to stand clear of the doors. In Yuma, the train filled up again, but in Carrie's dream it was no longer a train, but a large metal car, with the low rumble of an engine purring away in some unseen compartment. Las Vegas blurred past, as Vegas has been known to do. Then, Carrie saw the San Francisco skyline materialize out of the fog. "I'm there," she thought to herself. And then, "I'm here. Time to wake up."

Carrie came out of the airport doors with her single trunk loaded on a cart, looking for the BART signs. She hoped to get to Antioch in time to catch the bus, to avoid the cost of a rideshare on the last leg. As she dragged her belongings onto the yellow line, she thought she heard a coin drop on the floor. She paused, looking for the source of the sound. It defied her search at first, and she gave up in favor of wrangling her trunk into a secure place out of the aisle. After the doors closed, the train started to move, and she had slid partway into the nearest seat, she spotted it against the far wall: It was a ring. Small, delicate, with rows of tiny diamonds sparkling around a clear, brilliant center stone.

She looked around, but didn't see a likely source for the item, so she stepped across, knelt and picked it up. Standing, Carrie continued to look for the owner, someone who would certainly miss this beautiful piece of jewelry. A young woman in the seat next to hers caught her eye. There was something familiar about this person, although Carrie was sure she'd never seen her before. She was petite, pretty, but seemed somewhat disheveled in a way that Carrie could not at first identify. The woman was staring at her hands in her lap, where she was absently massaging the fingers of one with the other. Carrie could just make out the narrow tan line on the ring finger.

Sitting down, she faced forward and held the ring up in front of her own face, as if simply admiring it, nothing more. Without looking, the stranger in the next seat said, "I don't want it."

Carrie could hear her own voice coming out of the woman's mouth. There was a split second in which she wanted, impulsively, to throw the ring back on the floor, perhaps even stomp on it. She wanted to take sides with her new friend, to align with her, absorb some of the pain that was already starting to leak through what was left of that mascara.

"Then sell it."

The woman turned to look up at Carrie. She didn't say anything, just made eye contact. It was a span of only a few seconds, but it was filled with the sounds of train whistles, horse hooves on cobblestone streets, and the smells of bourbon and diesel. There were willow trees with hard, cold benches, and dried ham wrapped in stolen parchment. There were tired nights, sore backs, other passengers coming and going, torn dresses, dirty hems, and sweat. Then there were tears. Lots of them, old and new.

Carrie saw the young woman reach up slowly and take back her ring. The look in her eye, still clouded in a mantle of anguish, also held a spark of something else. Carrie recognized the look, even if she could not name it. They rode together in silence as the train passed under the bay, emerging from the tunnel to a remarkable lack of fog.

"This is my stop," the woman said at the Oakland Station. She made no move to get up, and the train started moving again. She watched the city outside the window, blurring into flat lines of gray concrete streaked with traffic lights, and eventually giving way to the green and gold shimmer of the Berkeley hills. Once they were safely over the mountain she added, "I have a friend in Concord."

When the train stopped, the two sisters parted ways. Carrie and her trunk continued their voyage to Antioch. "Grit," she whispered to herself. "That's what that look is called, grit."

* * *

It was evening in Stockton, and the orchard was unseasonably warm and sweet in the early spring air. "A perfect night for a bonfire," Carrie spoke aloud to the pear trees, full blooms poised like frozen pompoms of a thousand cheerleaders.

She was overheard by the host, who happened to stroll into the scene at that moment. "It is." He pulled up to a stop near the burn pile, chuckling slightly. Then, looking at the well-prepared stack of kindling and firewood, he added, "Isn't that your trunk?"

Carrie sighed. "Yep."

The host was used to boarders of interesting habits, but this was a new one. He looked like he was trying to compose another question, so Carrie explained.

"I won't need it. I'm not going back."

"You could probably sell it. We have tenants come through all the time, probably take it off your hands right away. Nice steamer trunk like that…"

"Not interested." Carrie, waved her hand, wearing a wry smile that said, "You really won't talk me out of this."

The host shrugged, continuing on his way as Carrie lit the fire.

She watched the flames curl up around the edge of the trunk, licking away the wounds, scars, and sticky sap of a distant world. Carrie took a breath. Like watching the last lap of a horse race, all bets riding on the leader, with the finish line in sight. She exhaled. The whole thing slipped a bit, to a small shower of sparks. It cocked to a new angle as some of the burned kindling turned to ash and stopped supporting the weight of the trunk. The house, her old home, with all its contents, and the car, the pool—all the things she chose to not take—were starting to twist out of existence. The fire continued its seductive work, orange and yellow arms caressing the trunk, opening the sides, burning through the lid, pulling the whole thing down, bending it toward the ground. Carrie leaned forward, appreciating the heat of the fire on her face, opening her mouth to feel it on her tongue, to taste the toasted air, scoured clean in the fire.

The sun had gone down, and the orchard was coming alive with the stealthy movements of small night creatures. At this very moment, there were probably the eyes of a racoon, or a possum, or a feral cat, watching her from the branches, but Carrie would not look away, mesmerized by the spectacle of this abandoned trunk, helplessly melting into the ash, into the earth.

"Nope," she said. "Not going back."

The Black Heart

I was seventeen when I realized I had a grandmother. By that, I mean one day it dawned on me that my mother had a mother. Obviously, I'd always known that she must have had one, but I hadn't really thought of her ever having been a child. It had not occurred to me that my mom—beautiful, confident, compassionate, intelligent—had once been a girl, like me. I was a senior in high school at the time, and I was very shy, self-conscious, and had mediocre grades. My mother was always supportive, patient, and kind. She was my hero. Even if I didn't say it out loud, I knew she was the woman I wanted to be, and I felt that she had always been so. I struggled to grasp the idea that she had not always been exactly as she was right now, that she had been younger in some remote past. All of these thoughts came to me, over the course of perhaps ten seconds, when she told me the news: her mother had passed away.

Before I could think about my words I remarked, "I didn't know she was still alive." I immediately regretted saying this.

However, my mom just smiled. "I know," she replied, "I don't talk about her much." I remained silent, processing. Then she added, "I don't think you would remember her. You were just a baby the one time she came to see us in California."

I admitted that I had no recollection of my grandmother. For that matter, I had grown up having only sparse contact with any of our relatives on her side. My mother's family all lived on the east coast, and I had only met a few of them when they came to California for a visit. I always assumed it was just too far for us to travel and that's why we never made it back to North Carolina. I had heard stories about quite a few aunts, uncles, and cousins, so I knew they existed. At that moment, however, I was not really thinking about those distant relations. I was still trying to reconcile the woman before me with the image of a child, a little girl, a teenager. It was a lot to process.

"Did you go to high school back east?" It seemed like the obvious question.

She smiled again, nodding. "I went to school in Swannanoa," she said. "Community High."

"Did you get good grades?"

Now she laughed. "No."

Suddenly, I began to cry. I didn't know why at the time, and thirty-five years later I'm still not sure. Perhaps it was just overwhelming, the thought that my mom went to high school, like me, and that she may have had some of the same problems I had. Or maybe I felt sorry that, knowing she did have a mother, her loss must be terrible. Or it could have been the realization that someday I would lose her—that this concrete form of strength and endurance, love and light would be gone. It's possible that some deep, primal instinct in me was reacting to the death of a family member: a direct ancestor, so close in the blood line. Yet I don't recall thinking about any of these things. My mind was fixed on the thought of my mother once being like me, and the corollary of me being like her. It was a bit of a shock to my teenage brain.

I remember how it felt, her hugging me, holding me through my sobs, cooing over my shoulder like one would with a child. She asked no questions, and I felt that answers would not matter anyway. I was sad, and that's all she needed to know. It was her way, and I had come to count on it. In another flash, I envisioned myself, decades older, doing the same for a child of my own. I only hoped I would be as good at it as my mother had always been for me. That thought sobered me up a little—the idea that I could ever be the caliber of woman as the one who held me now. I wiped my nose on her upper arm and stepped free, thankful for who she was.

She glanced at her damp sleeve and said, "Well, thanks for that!" We both laughed, and my brief moment of gloom evaporated as quickly as it had begun.

So, mom flew to North Carolina. It was one of the few times that I can remember Cinny Halverson riding on a plane. Nobody else went with her. She had insisted that my little brother Rudy and I stay home with Dad.

I don't recall asking, but somehow my father got to talking about the North Carolina clan. We were in the kitchen, cleaning up after dinner. My brother had gone to his room.

"I'm not sure," my dad explained, "but I think your mother is one of the few left in that part of the family. Except for Gramma Teri's ex-husbands, the only family members are a few cousins, mostly second. I'm not sure how many of them even met Gramma."

"Is Gramma Teri spelled T-E-R-I, or T-E-R-R-I-E?" I really didn't care, but I figured it was something I should actually know.

"T-E-R-I." He was silent for a minute. "I think one of mom's aunts is still around. It seems like Bethanie was alive not too long ago. I could be wrong about that."

"Have I met Aunt Bethanie? I thought she was your sister."

"That's Aunt Beth - Elizabeth. She's been out to visit, although it's been a few years. You've met your cousin Kathy, too. That's Beth's daughter. But Bethanie has never been out to see us in California. She's your grandmother's oldest sister."

"I think I remember mom talking about her."

"She may have, but more likely you heard about her other aunt, Madison." He smiled briefly, then added, "You wouldn't remember her, either."

"Madison." This sounded familiar. "Aunt Matty?"

My father sighed, as though relieved to hear the name. "Yes." He said, "Your mother spent a lot of time at Aunt Matty's house." Pause. "She passed away when you were still little." He handed me another dish. I began to dry it. "In fact, I'm surprised mom's going to the funeral at all, without Matty there. The only time your mother's travelled back to Carolina was to see her aunt. Mom never had much use for her mother."

Deep down, I knew this, although I had no specific information on the subject. I asked, out of curiosity more than anything, "Did they not get along?"

My father sighed again, deeply, before answering. "Gramma Teri was married six times," he said. "Not all of them wanted children."

I acted like that made sense to me, but it did not. He didn't offer any more information.

* * *

Cancer took my mother from us when I was thirty-five. It was three weeks before her sixtieth birthday. She died at home, in her own bed, with my father at her side. She looked so small, and fragile. A thin pale image, like a creased and faded photograph of my mother, resembling her only enough to remind us of the lively, robust woman she had once been. In her last five years, she remained the guiding light for my brother and me. I had been through a bitter divorce, and she was supportive as ever—my cheerleader, my confidant. Rudy had been in and out of rehab several times, with our mom forever offering words of encouragement, never giving up on him long after the rest of us had.

There had been numerous trips to the hospital, usually for pneumonia or liver problems—the special gifts of radiation and tamoxifen. In between these valleys on the descending path of my mother's health there were a few better periods, which somehow seemed to coincide with holidays. My children were very small then, but they remember fondly the Christmas mornings at Grammy's, the Easter egg hunts, the Thanksgivings with our small family (and usually a few friends). She would prepare a festive meal as she always had, until the last year or so. Then, I took over the cooking. She would supervise, perched on a barstool, directing me through the traditional family dishes. She did not want to die with our beloved recipes locked inside her head, and she made it clear that this was my training.

My mother's cousin Tracy flew out right away to help with the arrangements. Aunt Bethanie's daughter was energetic, sharp, and very well organized. She reminded me of my mother, which was both comforting and distressing, depending upon the moment. We decided to schedule a service on the Sunday before Christmas, with a wake at my parent's home in the afternoon. It was sunny but chill outside, which was unfortunate as we quickly ran out of space in the house once guests arrived, and very few of them seemed willing to brave the December air out on the deck. I was not prepared for the number of friends and family that had come from all over to be here. I found myself wandering through the crowded house, mumbling, "Thank you" in response to the condolences coming at me from all sides, mostly spoken by faces I did not know and would never remember. I was rescued by Tracy.

"Show me Cinny's room." It was a command, not a request. I jumped at the opportunity to exit gracefully in the company of the one relative I actually knew. I led the way upstairs, feeling the whispered din fading to black behind us. I closed the door, blotting out the last of the distant voices with a decisive click. We stood together for a moment, just inside the door of my parents' bedroom.

"She died right there." I pointed at the bed, neatly made, with colorful shams and several well-worn books on the otherwise empty nightstand.

Tracy sat down on the end of the bed, bouncing just a tiny bit, as though testing it for comfort. It seemed a little comical, this playful turn from a woman in her seventies, and I giggled softly. I felt relieved to be so removed from the party, alone with Tracy in my mother's private space. I took the lounger next to the window, feeling the sunlight glowing through the sheer curtains, warming the inside of the glass like a comfortable, welcoming greenhouse.

"Ruby's sober now," Tracy said, a statement that called for confirmation.

"Yes," I answered. "I don't know if she stayed alive so she could see it, or if he cleaned up so he could be with her before she went, but he's got, like, six months now, I think."

"That's good." She was thoughtful. "Too many of us have stayed on that path too long."

"Are there other alcoholics in the family?"

"You don't know, do you?" Tracy's eyebrows raised just a touch, mildly surprised. I didn't respond right away, so she answered on her own. "Your mother didn't talk about her family."

"Never."

"When she was a girl, Gramma—my grandmother, that is—sent my Aunt Matty to take your mom away from Aunt Teri."

I sat for a moment, reconciling that with the few bits of information I already had. "Yes," I said. "My dad told me she'd spent a lot of time with Aunt Matty."

Tracy nodded her head. "I was sixteen, so she would have been four at the time." She seemed to stare off into space for a bit. "I wasn't really aware of what was going on. I was in high school, and things weren't that great at my house, either. I know that Teri didn't put up a fight, though, when Matty showed up demanding to take her kid."

"No?"

"Not really. She turned around and got married to her new drinking buddy, then disappeared for a few years."

"Dad said Teri was married a lot, but didn't elaborate."

Tracy chuckled, then said in singsong voice, "Always a bride, never a bridesmaid. That's what they"— she stopped, suddenly looking at something across the room.

I tried to follow her gaze, but I couldn't determine what had pinned her attention. "What?" I asked, looking back at her expression. Tracy was smiling slightly, a little wistfully, I thought.

"Sorry," she shook her head. Then she stood and stepped over to the vanity. "It's just, this was Aunt Matty's." She picked up an ornamental jar from the table, and sat down in the dressing chair, swiveling to face me. "I remember it from her house."

The familiar vessel was not part of the vanity set. It could have been a vase, I thought. It was square in footprint, and roughly the size of a wine bottle. However, it had a large lid that screwed into the top with wide threads cut from the glass. It was obviously intended to hold something, but there was no indication of what that could be. The face of the jar was curved slightly inward, in contrast to the shape of the sides and back, which bowed outward a little. Hand-applied to the front of the jar was a large heart, made of deep, liquidy black glass, hanging on the crystal clear jar as though it floated in the shimmering air.

When I was younger, I had thought the heart might be made of obsidian. I was fond of the idea that such a thing might have been forged in the fires of an ancient volcano, cooling lava revealing its shape in some primeval landscape: a heart, waiting for countless millennia to be discovered. As an adult, I realized it was really the handiwork of a talented glassmith, pouring their skill and love into the artwork for us to admire, standing out from among the various decorations displayed upon the vintage toile of the dresser. I suddenly remembered where I had first seen the jar.

"I think," I began. "I think mom brought that back from North Carolina. It was when she went to Gramma Teri's funeral."

Tracy remained silent for a long moment. Then she nodded, saying, "That makes sense. When Aunt Matty died, Aunt Teri ended up with most of her sister's stuff." She paused again, then shook her head, adding, "Your mother never attended Teri's funeral." My astonishment must have shown, and Tracy held up a defensive palm. "Oh, she was there at the house," she said, "visiting with family, wishing condolences, and all of that. But she was not at the service."

"She never talked about it. I didn't ask."

"Why would you?" Tracy shrugged, setting the jar back on the table. "But truth be told, Cinny did not travel across the country to pay respects to her mother. She came to see us." Then she pointed at the jar, adding, "And to get that jar, apparently."

We sat in silence for a few minutes, both exploring memories, revising them slightly in the new light glinting from the black heart jar.

As if on autopilot, I stood slowly, retrieved the jar from the vanity. A plan, still half formed, was leading my feet. "Come on," I declared. Tracy rose and followed me back to the living room. I passed through the mob of guests, politely acknowledging whatever they may have said, and decided that my destination was the kitchen. I turned halfway around and leaned into Tracy. "Go to the Christmas tree," I instructed her, "and grab the present labeled 'Cinnamon.'" She nodded and veered in that direction.

In the kitchen, I set the jar down and quickly gathered a few things. By the time Tracy showed up, I had opened the jar and placed it on a cookie sheet in the middle of the kitchen table.

"What is this?" Tracy was referring to the present she carried. "Was this something you got for your mother before…" She trailed off.

"It *is* my mom." I chuckled, with a wry grin. "Her ashes," I explained to an obviously confused Tracy. "I was wrapping presents, and she was sitting right there by the table…so I wrapped her!" Tracy began to grin as she caught on. "One second. I'll be right back." I said, stepping to the kitchen door. I spotted my father not far away. "Dad!" I called, in a loud undertone. "Find Rudy," I said, "and come in here." He looked around, then headed into the crowd. I turned back to Tracy. "Go ahead and open it."

By the time my dad came in, followed by my little brother, we had peeled the wrapping paper from the box, opened it, and removed the plastic bag of ash from inside. He took in the scene at a glance and started to tear up. "Perfect," he said, his voice husky with emotion. "It's perfect."

Tracy now had the bag open. I handed him a spoon. "Care to start us off?" I asked, and he nodded.

Thus began a process that lasted about twenty minutes. I spooned some ash into the jar next, whispering a few words to my mother as I did so. Then my brother and Tracy followed suit. There were already a few relatives in the kitchen, and they wanted to participate in this ad hoc ritual, so we encouraged them. Word had gotten out to the living room, and soon there was a line at the door, friends and family, cycling through the kitchen. It was suddenly quiet, save the whispers of those at the black heart jar.

I could overhear most of them from my place at the table. I recognized stories from mom's childhood, and names of people she had known. I learned about her illness in seventh grade and the way she inspired others in sports. Someone I did not recognize told her to finish college in heaven, then turned briefly to me and explained that mom had been granted a much sought-after scholarship, but moved to California before she could complete the program. There were words of thanks, apologies, hopes and dreams, terms of endearment, and notes of goodwill. One person used the moment to whisper a joke, and I could almost hear my mother's laugh ringing back from somewhere inside the jar. Eventually Dad, Tracy, and I poured the last of my mother into her new home, filling the jar completely. I screwed on the lid and carried it into the living room, parading to the Christmas tree while holding my mother before me.

I turned to face the crowd, lifted the glass urn aloft, and stood still for a moment, waiting to see if anyone would look away. The last whispers trailed off.

"Here is what remains," I spoke in a low tone that carried easily through the silent room, "of Cinnamon Margaret Halverson, known simply as 'Cinny' to most of you." I handed the jar to my father, who immediately lifted it high, and started moving through the packed living room toward the fireplace. I continued. "The black heart jar was very special to her," I found myself speaking, finishing the impromptu ceremony, "and has become her final resting place. I know she is now reunited with her lost loved ones, as we all shall be in our own time." My father placed the jar upon the mantel, reverently, tears flowing unchecked down both cheeks.

* * *

I recently received a letter from Tracy, my first cousin once removed, and the only living human with meaningful memories of my mother's childhood. I had been in correspondence continuously with Tracy since mom's funeral, fifteen years before. We had gotten to know each other well, and through her perspective (she was a decade older than either of my parents) I came to better understand some of the anecdotes and family histories I had been told.

In the letter, Tracy explained that her health was slowly deteriorating, but she was hoping to feel a little better before cooking for the family on her eighty-sixth Christmas. It sounded like something my mom would have said. She went on to convey some of the latest news, and to ask about my "children," of whose ages she never seemed to be very clear. But she also told me something new, an observation she had apparently never thought to mention before. Among everything else in a note of two handwritten pages, was this simple statement:

> *"You know, your mother never hated Teri. She didn't understand her, she didn't approve, and she must have felt that she was unfortunate to have such a neglectful, deceitful, ungracious woman for a mother, but she never hated her. Aunt Matty taught her better than that. She spent*

fourteen years under Matty's roof, until she married your father and left for California. She was already pregnant with you, and I think she just wanted to make sure that her mother never saw you. Not out of hate, but caution. She wanted to protect you."

I set the letter down and sipped my tea for a few moments. The idea that my mother would be compassionate for one who had wronged her had the ring of truth. Saying that it even applied to Teri only proved the point. I set the cup down and penned a response.

After wishing her the best of health, answering questions, and sharing a small amount of gossip, I finished the letter with the following thought:

"I suppose I have always known that my mother was not capable of hate, but I am glad to see you putting it into words. I will disagree with you on one point, however: she certainly did not have a neglectful, deceitful, ungracious woman for a mother. She had Aunt Matty, and that was the only real mother she ever knew."

I dropped the letter into the postal box on the corner and came back into the house. I prepared another cup of tea and sat at the kitchen table. Even after so many years, I still missed my mother's smile. I missed her hugs, her sense of humor, and the way she made me feel. Her encouragement had gotten me through more than one difficult semester, and had kept me in the game when I was sure I was out. The most challenging obstacles always seemed to shrink in her presence, as though the very darkness was afraid of her light. My mother had the kind of grace and beauty that other graceful, beautiful people only wish they had. More than that, anyone who remained in her company long would come to realize that, in fact, they had it, too. That's the woman I grew up with.

My children are grown now, with their own lives. I hope that they feel the same way about me as I do about the woman who showed me how to love them. In turn, I hoped that my mother had known how much I would appreciate the woman who taught her about love. By that, I mean her mother—her real mother—my Gramma Matty.

White Mouse and Charlie Part II

> *"When in the heart a mighty dread abides,*
> *Though well assured it cannot be fulfilled,*
> *The fear remains. I fear exceedingly,*
> *Nor can I trust myself unto myself."*

— *Seneca, "Oedipus, Act 1,"* FJ Miller translation

3 | Stops and Keys

My imaginary father looked annoyed. "Yeah, well, that's a fine tale," he said, "but it doesn't really change anything, does it?"

"No." I agreed. "The two enemies are evenly matched. How do I defeat White Mouse? That's my question."

"A noble effort, to be sure." I couldn't tell if he was sneering, or laughing in sympathy. "The triumph of good over evil." His voice had the sing-song sound of one who is repeating a fairy tale. But his expression changed when he asked, "What happens if Charlie wins this fight?" He seemed more genuine now, I could not detect any sarcasm in his question. "What happens then. exactly?"

I hadn't really considered this question in any detail. Of course I wanted Charlie to win, obviously. Charlie was the benevolence, truth, hope, kindness, generosity, compassion, love, and everything that was good. There was no question that he should be the victor, I was only concerned with how to accomplish this. Now my father was asking what it would be like. If I could exorcise the demon, what would be left? I decided I needed to continue the story.

The tense moment lasted long. Seasons may have come and gone, and perhaps mountains eroded to desert dust; we cannot say. Like a photograph of a magnificent lightning strike, intense, bold, energetic, frozen in flight, poised in that moment before comes the death and destruction. For Charlie, everything in the peripheral field slowly dimmed into a dull blur, such that the skyline glow of the pre-dawn twilight felt somehow softer, not so cold. The gate faded to non-existence behind him, as did the machinery noises beyond it. The grassy grounds to each side of the path were indistinct, like hopeful clouds of green firmament, and the indigo sky evaporated into the black.

At length, even the faces of the two opponents were fading. In the darkness, there existed only their eyes, boring into each other. Charlie's black orbs, planets suspended in space, interlocked with the two crimson lamps of the White Mouse face, glowing drops of blood in the empty night. There was nothing else, just the silent stare-down of mortal enemies, like the children's game, eternal, universal, a pure combat of the mind, played on the internal battlefield that is the interface of psyche and body, where the first to cave in to reflex is the one to lose.

But White Mouse, by apparently having no eyelids, is a cheat, and Charlie knew it. The long moment, like the slow "crack!" of a shot in the dark, was interrupted in the blink of an eye. And as he closed them ever so briefly, Charlie saw the surrounding world spring back into focus. The fence, the path, the wall, and a dozen copies of White Mouse, crystal clear, gleaming in the first rays of sun. In that instant, he formed a plan. Charlie and his antagonist were perfectly matched in strength, speed, and dexterity. For any measure, they were equals, and neither could win a fair fight. But White Mouse did not, by any means, fight fair (as we have seen in the illicit self-clones.) So, the question Charlie considered was, "What would White Mouse do in this situation?"

As his eyes opened, Charlie stepped forward, raising his sword high. It was a bold move, which would create a powerful strike of the sword, though leaving his body exposed for a brief moment as he released his defensive posture. White Mouse saw this and jumped at the opportunity. He kept his sword level, drawing his elbow back to thrust, point first, to skewer Charlie on the emotionless spit of arrogance.

But Charlie's sword never descended from on high. Nay, this was never his intent. Instead, the raising motion continued overhead, arching back, with sword arm circling like a windmill, now behind the wielder. And as the arc continued, the sword became a counterbalance, the force of which Charlie transferred to his forward arm. As White Mouse was stepping in for the kill, he was met with Charlie's left paw, raising with all the force of the sword arm descending behind. In the moment before he died, White Mouse saw the dagger, like a snake striking at his throat, a deadly prick of the finely tapered point, driven by physics and ingenuity in the paw of his dear rival. Had White Mouse been capable of expression, he may have registered surprise, astonishment, admiration, approval, anger, grief, and—above all—pain. But instead, the blank face simply stared at Charlie as the rosy fire of his wicked eyes dissipated into the ether.

Charlie looked up, hearing a faint note sing through the air, piercing in its pitch, but low like the tuning of a piano string off in some distant hall. He was looking directly at the faces of the White Mouse copies that still surrounded him completely, destruction from all sides, menacing, emotionless, starkly beautiful in the golden hour cross light, empty Rembrandts on three-dimensional canvas. Suddenly, the tightening piano wire reached its limit and broke, with all of the White Mouse faces shattering like an explosion of milky glass, broadcasting razor shards that evaporated quickly in the face of the defender, becoming a tenuous mist which, in turn, sucked back into the damp earth, like worms in retreat of the light.

It was done. The epic battle was over, once and for all. White Mouse, miracle of miracles, was gone, along with his wearisome deliveries of rotten, diseased fruit, in the forms of anger, envy, resentment; his hideous songs of pain and loathing; howls in the midnight air; buckets of regret, pity, and guilt, left like warped flowers on endless May Days; gilded gifts of pride, greed and wrath, disguised as greeting cards from family and old friends. And then there were the lies. Constant exaggeration, fabrication, and deceit in all things large and small. Unnecessary lies, from which there could be no tangible benefit, tall waves persistently beating upon an honest, innocent shore. It was all gone now.

The Computer was already calming down, settling into the familiar rhythm of daytime activity: breakfast of thought, dinner of work and recreation, sleepy evenings barefoot on cool tile floors, with breezes bearing burdens of flowers and fresh bread through rusty screens on hinged windows in the pink and yellow sunset. There was a click and whir of complex clockworks, levers and bearings rocking to the magical forces of springs and weights, kinetic energies driving planetary motions of happiness, contentment, kindness and hope. The gearbox would shift, ringing soft chimes, announcing moments of humility, compassion, and faith. The limitless power of The Computer was matched only by the temperance of the guardian, the keeper of the keys, the protector of the kingdom.

Charlie stood for long moments in silent contemplation, sniffing the new air in calm deliberation. It was a different world now. He decided to leave his assigned post at the gate, because he could. Charlie walked the perimeter, inspecting the fortifications, checking the landscaping for signs of decay, all the while humming softly to himself in time with the mechanical rhymes of his ward. The song seemed comforting, in a way, but also empty, like a jar of air, stored in a musty cellar for countless centuries without being opened. He continued his rounds, feeling a sense of completion that he'd not experienced in his entire time as guardian of The Computer. We see him now, back at the gate, turning to look at the world he has always seen in a different light, then opening the gate and walking inside.

Charlie stepped over the threshold a new mouse. Dressed in the same uniform he'd always worn, with the same fastidious look, and visibly sharp of senses, precise in movement, deliberate in direction, exactly the same as ever: the consummate warrior. But as we step back, watching him from a little distance, we get a new impression, a qualitative difference, perhaps the undetectable aura of calm, like a fresh, new shadow cast upon the ground, replacing the old one, tired, and threadbare. Charlie walked through the outer layers of The Computer, where a countless array of levers and handles adjusted a network of shafts and pushrods, linked to the spinning apparatus of the inner works. Charlie kept walking.

Through the motor chambers, where the powerful but delicate dynamos turned, heavy coils of gossamer copper, humming at a frequency which was tuned to the life of the universe itself, the primal note of all existence, mirrored in the finely crafted device. Through a layer of memory banks, with their orderly rows of bits, after which had been modeled the abacus, the cribbage board, and the rosary, but with the capacity to read all of the real world into numeric abstraction. Through the logic centers, where a thousand symbolic decisions could be simultaneously created, like dandelion seeds of word and deed, each spawning a thousand new variations, moments to be acted upon in the next clock tick.

Eventually, Charlie wound his way to the action room. It was small. An office, really, with concealed uplights at the edges revealing only a gently curving surface of smooth plaster. At one end, the console was flanked by rows of ticking teletypes, ticker tapes, and a single, large kinotrope puffing quietly to itself. Data from the logic centers, Charlie knew, came this way in a constant stream, activating the manuals on what had become known as the "Wurlitzer." This was supposed to happen by way of a "player," the personification of a system that we might think of as the amygdala of The Computer: the emotional element, the random voice in this otherwise sterile machine. Today, there was no player. The bench was empty; the console was unattended.

Charlie sat down in the player's seat, hardwood worn smooth from past decades of use, but cold from recent loneliness and neglect. His paws absently came up to touch the manuals, which he did not know how to play. Charlie reached out to the rows of ebony knobs along the head of the cabinet, each labeled in a foreign language, inscrutable, vacant. Neither the stops nor the keys were of any use to Charlie, and he felt that loss. But it was comfortable here, and The Computer was safe now—very little to do. A vacation seemed in order, and Charlie began to relax, the soporific rhythm of the machinery quietly lulling him into a meditative state. A tiny spider appeared near the right-paw edge of the console. It looked at Charlie for a few minutes, then began spinning a small web between one of the stops and keys.

4 | Replacement Fuse

"Huh." My father always had a way with words. He could express himself with refined eloquence when he wanted to. Unfortunately, he rarely wanted to. It was clear that he was not planning to offer any substantive comment.

"Well?" I asked. "Is that what you were looking for?" I was not feeling any more enlightened than I had at the beginning of this experiment. It seemed like a good time to just give up.

He remained silent for a few minutes, and I followed his example. Eventually, he responded with yet another question.

"What if White Mouse wins?"

The tense moment lasted long. The uncompromising seconds between clock ticks could be felt, perhaps even seen as tangible objects, stationary. A row of stone soldiers in a war memorial's arrested march. For White Mouse, the world became crystal clear in that moment. Facing Charlie —enemy, cousin, rival, unwanted friend—White Mouse could feel the black, glistening eyes reaching out to his own, softly groping, searching for a non-existent soul behind the rose-tinted windows of his own pale face. The grass beneath his hind paws seemed frozen in the cool pre-dawn air—not cold, really, but very still. A painted scene under an indigo sky.

Another tick of the second hand, and White Mouse realized what struggle must be going on for Charlie. Amidst their battle, poised to strike, he would be waiting to learn both his own fate and the fate of his interlocutor. The action had devolved into this child's game, a staredown, forfeit by the first one to blink. It was silly, purposeless: an inactive moment serving only to allow competitors time to plot and prepare. White Mouse always considered himself prepared and never felt the need to blink.

But Charlie did. The thirsty eye of any warm-blooded mammal will come to demand a response, and eventually each of Charlie's soft, brown lids closed briefly over its black, liquid lens. Only for an instant, but it was enough, and White Mouse sprang into action. Drawing an elbow quickly back, he lunged forward, throwing all his weight behind the paw that held his cutlass. As Charlie's eyes flicked open, he spotted the move and reflexively raised his own blade, managing to deflect the oncoming steel away from his most vital organs. But the flow of the force was only turned, not halted. The flat, angular object skipped, surfing the crest of Charlie's own sword for a long, spark-filled instant, then briefly airborn, it buried itself in Charlie's shoulder.

Charlie howled in anguish, twisting away, tearing the offending weapon out of the grip of White Mouse, clutching at it with his other paw as his own sword arm hung limp by his side. The blade was stuck, half its length protruding from the back of Charlie's shoulder and defying all attempts to dislodge it. White Mouse stood watching, calculating, estimating, sizing up his opponent, whose flailing was slowing with shock, fatigue, and loss of blood. In time, Charlie leaned sideways against the gate, slid to the ground, and sat there in an awkward heap, panting, a skewered roast, ready for the spit.

When it was clear that Charlie was down for the count, no longer struggling, impotent, White Mouse walked casually in, stood directly in front of the red-spattered pile of mouse in the walkway. He slowly took the handle in his right paw, placing the other on Charlie's collarbone, and withdrew the sword in a single, steady motion, releasing the howling all over again. The victor straightened up, looked at his fallen enemy for a moment, then casually stepping over Charlie's useless sword where it had fallen, he turned and strolled away into the wood.

Charlie, quite dazed, looked around. His world seemed small, and lonely. The computer careened recklessly in the cross light of the golden hour, metallic ringing from the overworked bearings and gimbles, sucking sounds of oil cups running dry, and the low vibration that seemed to emanate from some deep recess in the center—the heart and soul of the machine— struggling to understand this new and appalling chapter. Sometime during the clash, Charlie realized the extra copies of White Mouse had disappeared. When was that? They had been there at the start of the face-off, perhaps a dozen of them, arrayed in a menacing semi-circle, ready to attack. But they were gone now, it seemed, or perhaps they were never really there in the first place—only another special treat from White Mouse's bag of tricks.

Speculation was interrupted by the sound of softly crunching footsteps on the thawing grass. White Mouse walked directly up to Charlie, who had not moved at all, and leaned in close. He didn't look at Charlie's face, but examined the shoulder wound briefly. Then, with no warning at all, he clapped a paw directly onto the gash. There was an astonishing instant of delayed pain, like a cloudburst filling the night sky, a million raindrops frozen in the silent flash of lightning, then the thunderclap and a deluge of agony that washed Charlie into oblivion.

Charlie dreamed that an army of bees swarmed around him. Not threatening, but wholly benevolent, helping him to his feet as a team, and supporting him as they led him to the water. The bees fashioned clothing for him, out of wax. They made a scarf, and a pair of gloves, then they tied the two together, so that the gloves could not become lost. Charlie laughed, and the bees all turned to look at him. "Idiot mittens?" He said, "you've made me idiot mittens? I love them so much!" The bees made no comment, returned to their work. "I love you so much, too," Charlie added, "Thank you!" The dream faded to a scene of Charlie lazing in a rowboat, gently swaying on a moonlit pond.

It was twilight when Charlie woke. Not the dawn twilight he last remembered, but sunset. After some time, Charlie decided it was not actually the same day. He looked around, only to discover he was inside the gate, at the guardian station, lying on his own cot. He had not yet started to speculate on this when he tried to move and noticed some restriction: he could not use his right arm at all, and attempting to do so was entirely painful. Memory of the confrontation came back to him, and Charlie began to examine his condition.

To his surprise, he found that his shoulder had been bound with cloth strips, partially covering what appeared to be clay packed around the wound. More cloth had been looped around his neck, fashioning a sling for the affected arm. Lastly, Charlie saw that his paws were also bound, layered in cloth, neatly tied. This perplexed him, and he began the difficult process of removing the wrapping—mummy paws groping at each other. The inconvenience of this activity made Charlie realize their purpose: bound fingers could not undo the dressing of the wound, preventing damage while he slept. Charlie dozed off again.

In a remote future, Charlie would look back on this day as one of the most peaceful times of his entre life. The dissociation of constant pain drove his mind away from the material world, allowing him to sleep undisturbed. For similar reasons, he was not hungry, only drinking the occasional taste of water from a soft canteen that mysteriously appeared beside his bed. Charlie didn't often think about the battle, but when he did, it was with relief rather than sorrow. His injury released him of guardian duty; therefore the worrisome whine of The Computer was no longer his concern. Charlie felt, for the first time, free.

As days disappeared into weeks, Charlie adjusted to his new life, forming new routines, learning new ways of doing things. What was once his station became his home, and his habits led away from the gate itself, away from the haunts of White Mouse. On a spring day, several months removed from the fight, Charlie was in the garden, tending tiny green seedlings. He marveled at the way they imperceptibly moved toward the sun, toward unfettered life—rooted but limitless. He clutched at the watering can in his right paw but shifted to the left to raise it. It was a habit formed of resignation, the realization that, although fully healed, the severed tendons would never be able to lift that arm again.

White Mouse didn't seem to notice any of this. He had removed the rain cover from the eastern half of The Computer, presumably to encourage the sun, who was bringing heat and energy into the electromechanical core. Parts from the logic flow regulators were lying on the ground where they had landed when the primary assembly casing had disintegrated. Apparently White Mouse did not consider the system essential or worth repair, and grass was growing around the tarnished fragments. A new vibration had started, weeks ago now, coming from somewhere near the fluctuation dampers, possibly due to bearings that were damaged through excessive heat. Charlie did not engage. All of this was out of his paws now; the weight no longer rested on his shoulder.

One day, there was a loud popping sound, and the warm glow from inner chambers of The Computer suddenly went dark. The mechanical rumblings continued, of course, but the life-light was out, the circling of orbs and rocking of levers were simply going through the motions, dancers performing in an empty theater. Charlie watched from just inside the gate, seated in the guardian bench that the victor had never claimed. White Mouse, walking briskly out from The Computer's innards, paused at the gate. For the first time in eons, he looked squarely at Charlie, the angles of his impassive face framing his glassy red eyes, an empty pair of brackets hovering briefly. Then, he turned and continued through the gate. Charlie looked back at The Computer, where a wisp of black smoke was curling up from one of the central blocks.

White Mouse returned moments later, and Charlie was startled to see that he was brandishing a sword. Even more, it was Charlie's sword, which had lain where it had fallen, so long ago now. But White Mouse was ignoring Charlie and heading directly into The Computer. Curiosity sparked, Charlie followed.

They walked through the outer layers of The Computer, past the countless array of levers and handles, and the vast network of shafts and pushrods, into the motor chamber. The giant dynamos turned, heavy coils of gossamer copper rotating diligently, humming at a frequency which was tuned to the life of the universe itself, the primal note of all existence. But no energy was flowing out of the chamber. Charlie saw the open panel on the far wall, with black scorch marks trending up from the top seam. That's where White Mouse was headed, and reaching it, he turned back, looking at Charlie as if to say, "Are you ready for this?"

Charlie understood, and moved into position at the disconnect switch. Reaching out with his good arm, he looked over his shoulder, made eye contact, and then pulled the lever down. Immediately, the hum stopped, and the dynamos began to falter. White Mouse quickly reached into the box and yanked the remaining section of the main breaker from its clamps. He then gripped the sword by the center, and with a single decisive motion, snapped it into place, gave it a quick tug to confirm it was seated, then jumped back and looked at Charlie.

Here, there was a pause. Charlie was concerned. What would happen? That breaker must have blown for a reason, and this replacement was no fuse at all. His mind reeled to contemplate the possible disaster to come should he turn that switch back on. But the dynamos continued to slow and would soon be too low to bring back online. The now sleeping Computer would die without immediate action. White Mouse continued to stare and took a step forward. It was a vaguely menacing gesture, but more like an expression of exasperation, as if to say, "Well? What are you waiting for?" Charlie closed his eyes, and pushed the disconnect back into the run position. There were sparks as the switch welded itself closed. There was no going back now. The familiar hum of the motor mechanism had returned.

Charlie and White Mouse stood for a long minute, looking around, and listening to the routine sounds of their sentient home. Tick, tock, tick, tock, like a metronome for measuring the music of thought, or a timebomb waiting for its turn at the helm. The Computer was online, and running in the same erratic, breakneck way it had been in the days and nights since White Mouse had taken over, with no obvious side effects from the recent repair. They stood another long minute. Several minutes, really. And then White Mouse turned to face Charlie. They could both smell it: the dry, acrid tang of electrical scorching, and the sickening burn of melting insulation. The worst fears were confirmed: The Computer would not last long, the mechanism would soon be aflame. In fact, the metal walls around them were already too hot to touch.

They left the motor chamber, turning inward, to the center of The Computer. They waved goodbye to the memory banks, brisk calculations landing and taking off again reflected in the bright rosary beads, counting the penitent hours of the final descent. Then, continuing into the logic centers, sniffing the vapor trails of systematic decisions blurring past in fits and sparks of self-destructive brilliance. They both knew this was the room they would miss the most, each mouse for his own reasons.

They wound their way to the action room, the small control center of mind, where the player could weave harmonies of passion, joy, and warm embrace, or discordant visions of doubt, shame, and reckless abandon. The soft lighting bent with the walls, melting into a domed ceiling of rough porcelain, like a weathered, featureless China bowl, or the lightly foxed pages of an ancient book. The console was surrounded with data sources—inputs transmitted from the reaches of The Computer, converging in this tiny hippocampus—ready to be formed and molded into action. The teletypes, ticker tapes, and massive kinotrope were blazing with furious impotence, data overload impossible to digest, spilling out onto the floor to melt like snowflakes on a campfire griddle.

The console, the "Wurlitzer" at the center of everything, stood empty at the end of the room. It seemed lonely but unapproachable, and had the quivering manner of a purring cat, or a fish on the shore. The carved wood of the player's seat was worn, soft, inviting, but Charlie could only look upon it with solid apprehension. There was no rationality left in the stops and keys. The manuals were menacing, a death's head grimace, ready to bite the paws and erupt in maniacal laughter.

White Mouse barely paused. Taking in the chaotic scene in a single glance, he leapt forward, stood on the bench like a bird of prey pausing in the air before the lethal dive. He then set upon the console with all four paws—pulling stops, pounding keys, raking his claws the width of the manual, leaning forward to clutch at the hoses that grew from the top of the cabinet. Charlie stood by, helpless to intervene, wringing his good paw in the air as the discordant wailing of The Computer became the only thing that mattered, the only thing left.

5 | The Lever of Possibility

My father was laughing now. "Well," he chuckled, "White Mouse really knows how to party."

"Hey, I really had no idea where the story was going until I was done!"

This was true. At some point during the telling, I felt like I was no longer in charge, that the two mice had taken over, running through the story on their own. I was just a spectator, dissociated from the action in a strange, dreamlike way. It was disconcerting, but at the same time cathartic. When my father spoke again, I was ready for him.

"I like the first one," he said. "Better to be bored to death than blow shit up!"

"I don't." I responded quietly, almost an undertone. "I don't like it at all."

I dipped my head, gathered my resolve, and pushed back against the annoying expectations of my imaginary father.

The tense moment lasted long. It was the kind of moment in which anything could happen, but never actually did.

The time came and then went. Still, they remained. The two enemies—cousins, brothers, foes—began to relax just a tiny bit, though they kept their weapons ready. They were evenly matched and they both knew it. A fight could last a minute or a year, there was no telling, and probably no meaningful outcome would be obtained. They were not to be distracted. It was a silent stare-down, two children on a playground that smelled of concrete and summer heat, surrounded by the chain link fence that kept them safe from unimaginable predators lurking in ambush.

But it was not summer: there was no concrete, the players were outside the fence, and neither were safe. As two pairs of eyes, black versus red, shot imaginary arrows into each other, praying for a lucky shot in a momentarily lowered guard, The Computer spun quietly in the background. The tone of the great machine was one of complacency. A familiar sound, like that of a sewing machine when one is making curtains, with long, straight runs of forgiving percale; it is soporific, mesmerizing—until the seamster gets careless and tacks a thumb to the work. No blinking here, just sword tips rising and falling ever so slightly, with breaths becoming synchronized as White Mouse and Charlie bonded in their animosity.

The stalemate was broken by an intense, blinding flash of light, a freeze-frame of two statue-warriors, locked in relentless combat. The flash was followed immediately by Thor's hammer, descending to the anvil of Earth, where it struck a ringing blow in the forest edge, just a stone's throw from the gate. By now, the two mice stood shoulder to shoulder, weapons raised against this new threat, allies in the face of a common peril. Smoke curling up from the trees marked the point of the lightning strike. The rhythm of The Computer had risen, the click of gears punctuating the cycles of planetary orbs swishing the air. The mice continued to stare into the smoke, shallow breaths coming quickly with trepidation. Their fears were shortly confirmed, as red-orange fingers laced their way up the lower branches, reaching for the canopy in thirsty exploration.

The forest fire would be upon them in an hour, maybe less. There was no time to think, talk, or plan: The Computer must be protected at all costs. To die separately, or survive together, there was never even a question. The enemy of my enemy is my friend, as the saying goes. Until the crisis fades, the truce prevails. The deer and the mountain lion, coyote and rabbit, bobcat and shrew, flee side by side from the wrath of the yellow, cackling, hissing flame. A treaty was formed, signed in the promise of unspent blood, to be ratified in battle and held in good faith until such time as it would no longer be needed.

But truce does not equal unity. Much to Charlie's dismay, White Mouse immediately began hacking at the fence with his sword, prying at the planks, popping them loose to dismantle the barrier. Charlie instantly abandoned the thought of putting a stop to that, as the top priority must be retrieving water from the cisterns. There was no time to waste on White Mouse. He ran toward the far end of the compound, looking somehow like a petty thief, running through town grabbing buckets, bottles and bags, suddenly valuable, worth any risk. He located a cart along the way and, reaching the reservoirs, began rapidly filling and loading his ragtag collection of containers. By the time he returned, the gate stood alone, while most of the adjoining fence sections had been dismantled. White Mouse was nowhere in sight.

Charlie parked the cart and ran back to the cistern, on the way collecting a wheelbarrow, along with numerous jugs, crocks and pots. This time around, the vessels were heavier, and much harder to manage. Most of them could not easily be dipped in the tank and had to be filled by ladling the water into them with a water can from the garden (which was the best thing available on short notice). Frantic, Charlie spent more than a little energy cursing White Mouse for abandoning him in this time of need. Only twenty minutes into this time of truce, and the fair-weather enemy had shown his true colors in crisis. Charlie's blood boiled at the thought.

But things appeared much worse when Charlie returned to the area of the gate, only to find the cart, with its supply of water, missing. He looked around in panic and found that all of the wooden fence planks had been scattered outside the perimeter like kindling. The iron gate stood there, like an impotent sentinel. What had once guarded the only ingress, was now merely a marker within a broad ring of open access. Charlie stood, aghast, feeling as though quicksand beneath his feet was drawing him under with the inevitable vertigo of abject failure. Then White Mouse ran into his field of view, quickly stealing the wheelbarrow.

This time Charlie ran after him. It was too much to bear. Any time Charlie gained working on his own was lost when White Mouse undermined his efforts. So, after a brief pause in shock, he followed. He was prepared to grapple with bare paws, being unsure of where he'd abandoned his sword in the emergency. He gained quickly upon the heavily laden White Mouse, who completely ignored Charlie. Perhaps it was fear of spilling all of the hard-earned water, or perhaps curiosity was creeping in, but Charlie ran alongside the wheelbarrow for a few moments instead of attacking. They followed the empty fence line around the perimeter, where the fire could be seen approaching the loose piles of planks so recently thrown. Some of them were already starting to burn. As they rounded the corner of the boiler shed Charlie spotted the cart of water, and he stopped in his tracks.

He watched White Mouse park the wheelbarrow next to the cart, near one of the buildings. It was on the back of the building, which had once abutted the fence. The barrier had been removed, its wooden parts thrown far away from the area of the structure. Further, the grass and dry leaves had been scraped away, leaving the earth nearly bare. Charlie felt his face flush with embarrassment, but his chest swelled with hope, driven by a heart full of new respect for his unorthodox yet wily companion. It was the coal shed, and the adjacent fence would have acted as a fuse for a firebomb that they could never have extinguished. As it was, with the kindling gone and plenty of water, the two mice could easily protect this critical vulnerability.

In fact, it took very little work to keep the fire at bay. A few buckets of water, and the occasional bit of stomping on embers, was all there was to it. The tide of flame rose to within a few feet of the other buildings, crossing the fence line like an orange wave, then receding into itself, leaving behind a black field of scorched earth, like a mudflat on the voiceless shore of a once blazing sea. The modest clear space around the coal shed proved defensible, and by afternoon the boil of activity sank to a simmer, and eventually became a period of stewing—the alert watch for embers that might have been carried their way by the strong updraft above the receding epicenter. The Computer, now winding down to an idle, was safe again.

Morning found White Mouse and Charlie slumped against the coal shed, blinking sleep from their eyes as a sepia sun peeked through the lingering layer of smoke to the east. Charlie took a sip from one of the remaining jugs in the wheelbarrow, and, after a pause, passed it to White Mouse. The Computer slept peacefully, remarkably catlike in a soft, glowing way, eyes closed, a delicate purring of happiness and restful abandon. As much as Charlie might wish to return to his comfortable routine, there was no point in guarding the now absurd gate. An inspection seemed in order. So, Charlie stood, stretched, cracked the knuckles of his interlaced paws, and walked in the direction of The Computer. White Mouse followed.

The two mice tramped the perimeter, viewing the gaps in the protective fencing, which had helped to save them by its very non-existence. (Thanks to White Mouse!) The mechanical whispers of The Computer became the soundtrack to their activity, and they strode to the rhythm of gold and platinum planets, orbiting between the crystal spires of the higher functions. From out on the grounds, the inner workings of The Computer were pure fantasy; mysterious shadows of movement wrapped in its vast collection of gears, wheels, levers and rods, all vibrating to the underlying baritone of the engines buried deep in the labyrinthine core.

Among the intricate systems of sensors and adjustment, White Mouse stood peering at one of the controls. It was a large, vertical lever, simply labeled

"Possibility." Charlie stepped forward, holding both paws up, the universal sign for "Don't touch that!"

White Mouse halted, his outstretched paw a few inches from the lever. There was a brief moment in which White Mouse, teetering on the brink of deliberation and intemperance, turned his expressionless face toward Charlie. Then, turning back to the lever, he grabbed it and quickly pulled it down. Not only did nothing happen, but the lever returned smoothly to its original position when released. They stood there looking at it for a moment, then at each other. With a pair of shrugs, they turned inward, passing through the outer layers and into the workings proper.

The dynamos of the motor chambers, full of bright copper and dark iron, held the mice captive for a moment. Distorted reflections on the polished silver walls leered back at them in mock disbelief. The mesmerizing drone, a continuous, emphatic "om," made the air sparkle with invisible power and the vague scent of ozone. Time passed, the spell relaxed, and the two mice moved on to the memory banks, pulsing with synaptic light in well-ordered chaos. If this was the vessel that held the wine of knowledge, the vintner was housed in the next room: the logic centers. At the threshold between the two, White Mouse and Charlie felt the unavoidable sense of awe one gets when witnessing that thing which is the measure of all other things. They also felt awkward, self-conscious, and more than a little intrusive, so they passed quickly through.

They now stood together at the door of the action room. It was a space so sacred that neither mouse had ever seen this door, much less the chamber beyond. They each placed a paw flat on the door and pushed it inward, rewarded by a slight gasp of escaping air and the satisfying slip of finely crafted hinges smoothly carrying the obstacle to one side. They entered together.

It was essentially an office, almond-shaped, with hidden lighting that directed up the gently curving surface of smooth plaster walls. At one end, the console was flanked by rows of ticking teletypes, telegraphs, and something that appeared to be a steam-powered kinotrope hissing in tiny puffs. Data from the logic centers clearly entered the action room in this way, surrounding the console with a constant stream of information. On the bench before the console sat the player, the interpreter of all things worth interpreting, who would act upon the manuals and controls before them. White Mouse and

Charlie both averted their gazes, as though hiding the scene from their own sight would somehow keep them from being noticed.

There was a period in which the two mice could have left without interaction. The player sat at his post, not moving, his empty face directed at the data streams. The Computer was clicking in a casual way all around them, but the sound could barely be noticed inside the action room. Everything remained in this equilibrium—eyes down, player motionless, The Computer clicking —for several minutes. It lasted until a specific pattern of information appeared before the player, calling for his action, like the emotional response of the amygdala and hippocampus centers. The player reached up with one hand, deftly flicking a few of the stops open. Then, in the same motion brought both hands down, one upon each of the two manuals, with a single cord of seven notes.

The chord only held for a few seconds, but it echoed in the ears of the two mice as they wandered absently out of the action room, through the logic centers, the memory banks and motor chambers.

Emerging from the outer layer, they sat down and rested together on the ground, watching the sun rising in the east. It was a new day, in more than one sense. Everything was fresh, washed clean, purified by the fire. Eventually White Mouse turned his face to Charlie, who felt he could read the expression in those liquid rubies: "I'm hungry."

Charlie considered this for a moment, then wondered how long they had been in there. "Not long," he thought to himself, and then, "I think I'm hungry, too."

The buzzing of a flying insect, alone and shy, drew Charlie back to his new reality. He sniffed the air cautiously, finding no imminent threat. The sun was up, the day had begun, all was going to be well. The Computer was booting to a world of birdsong and fresh flowers to the unscorched west, acrid smoke to the fire-ravaged east, with amber sunshine on naked trees whose shadows were lost on the blackened earth. But pyrocumulous clouds were dropping water to replenish the land and cisterns, while seeds awakened by heat and opportunity were already beginning to stir in the wake of the fire. Even as White Mouse and Charlie were considering their new course, there were clicking noises speaking to them from the lower structures of the machine. This—the measure of all things, the center of the known universe, the deep thoughts of all that is good, evil, neither or both—like a campfire starting from a few damp bits of driftwood and dry grass.

They stood and began to walk back around to the front of the compound. Survivors of a shipwreck, bedraggled, cold, optimistic as the sun warmed them on the beach of survival. They'd only taken a few steps when they were once again in front of the Lever of Possibility. White Mouse threw a glance over his shoulder at Charlie, but didn't wait for a response. He reached up swiftly and pulled the lever down. This time there was an audible "click," and the lever stayed in the new position. They both stared at it for a long moment, shrugged, and continued walking.

6 | The Empty Cup

I finished my story, my explanation, my excuses, while my imaginary father remained silent. I had been in a dreamland of sorts, a kind of trance induced by my own, longwinded story. As usual, I was afraid to meet my father's gaze. I sat looking at my coffee cup for a long time, as though I might find approval in the bottom of the empty vessel, but there was nothing there. Perhaps I needed something stronger than coffee, or maybe I was already drunk with success, as I could feel the inner struggle weakening with every breath, now that I had given voice to a truce between my warring thoughts.

"I think," I began, still looking into my cup, reluctant to raise my eyes, to face my father. But then I stopped midthought. What was I going to say? I might tell him that he was wrong, that I had never believed him anyway. Or I could say how much I loved him, and how I trusted his every word. Either would be equally true, but empty in this moment. I wanted to tell him I had outgrown him, that I truly did not need him anymore, although I would always take time to listen to his words and hold them close, like a well-worn map of places I'd already been. I would congratulate him on his success, and comfort him in his losses, because those are the things he should have done for me.

"I think," I began again, raising my head high. But the room was empty, he was nowhere to be found. I set the empty cup on the table; I would wash it in the morning. I stood up, absently turning out the light as I left the kitchen. It suddenly dawned on me that I would never hear my father's voice again.

Rose of a Purple Thorn

"I'm Nobody! Who are you?
Are you – Nobody – too?
Then there's a pair of us!
Don't tell! they'd advertise – you know!
How dreary – to be – Somebody!
How public – like a Frog –
To tell one's name – the livelong June –
To an admiring Bog!"
– Emily Dickinson, poem 260

Thorn

"Oh, hey," the stage manager's tone was contemptuous. "It's the other band."

"Thorn," I responded. "It's Thorn."

"Yeah, like I said. The other band."

I didn't want to make waves. I started to go back to my work, finagling our gear, getting ready to place it on stage once Black Heart's instruments were out of the way. The drum kit was already assembled in the crossover, ready to shove out through a curtain gap. Our electronics were stacked in the stage left wing, riding on the wheeled speaker cabinets. We were just tuning up and checking our batteries, chomping at the bit before we lost too much of the crowd.

The stage manager, I think his name was Ron, was on the same page but clearly reading the script differently.

"You sure you want to do this?" he asked, pointedly. "The headliners are done; the audience is walking out. It's after midnight, who do you expect to play for?"

I looked at the rest of the band. They had stopped what they were doing in a freeze-pose of kinetic equilibrium. Hands were reaching for the cymbal boxes, halting in the act like a thief in a spotlight. Wheels on amps were suddenly silent, the squeaking paused, like everything else. A guitar was in mid-flight, between the case and the shoulder of its master. In this motionless state, who could say which way it was going to move? Was the player taking it up? Or putting it away? Was this a still photograph of pre-game excitement, or a tired moment captured as the guitar longed for its case, a night creature seeking its coffin before daybreak. Tableau of musicians, a single Claymation frame, implications unclear. The band would act on my word. It was up to me to break the spell, and I was struck dumb.

Ron was getting impatient. "Hey," he verbally stamped his booted foot. "My guys want to clean up, go home. Are you boys gonna keep us here, or what?"

This was not getting easier. In fact, his words made me bristle: none of us in Thorn express any clear gender. It would be just as certain (and equally inaccurate) to call us "girls." Was this a good time to correct Ron's use of terminology? It was tempting. Nobody but Ron, the band,

and I was paying any attention. I could be polite about it, or not, it wouldn't matter—Ron would probably make life harder for us either way, if I pointed it out. At the same time, it could give me an out, if I pissed off the stage manager and we had to leave. It would take the responsibility off my shoulders, and that thought appealed to me in the moment.

And how could I ask the band to stay, anyway? Ron was right: it was late. Half the crowd was already gone. Sure, there was a small knot at the bar ordering drinks, so at least those people would be around for a little while anyway. The road crew was working rapidly to break down the last remains of Black Heart; the moment to move was imminent. I looked at the face of each of my fellow musicians. They wanted to leave; I could see it. Yet, somehow, I sensed that they were hoping for a reason to stay, that they were looking anxiously at me, ready to spring into action should I give them license.

I looked out on the floor, where a few scattered clumps of friends were laughing, chatting, finishing their drinks—the last stragglers of the post Black Heart exodus. There was a lot of empty space, and nobody seemed to be paying any attention to the stage at all. But then I noticed a chair, right in the middle of the dispersing crowd. It was a chair from the bar, and it supported a smallish human. With the stage lights in my face, I couldn't see much detail—hair color, how they were dressed, whether or not they were holding a drink—but I could tell they were looking at the stage, at us, at the band. They were waiting.

I turned back to the stage manager. "Fuck you," I said. "We're going on."

To my surprise, he smiled. "Okay." There was some annoyance in his tone, but at the same time, a touch of respect. Apparently, I had given him the right answer. "Rock on!" He gave an expansive, sweeping gesture, encompassing the stage, the lights, the speakers, and the band, who had been looking alternately at Ron and myself. Now that our little exchange was over, they sprang into action. I could feel the showtime exhilaration blast off as we slid into place, plugged in, and cranked up.

No sound check. We just started playing. We played to the person in the chair, forgetting everything else. That was the goal. If we could just reach one of our fellow humans, it would mean we did our job. If that person got up to dance, it would make the late gig worth our time.

And maybe, just maybe, if they stood up at the end, applauding our curtain call, we could call it a success.

So, we played a song for the smallish human in the chair. It was just a warm-up, our usual kick off. Nothing too elaborate, but a solid song nonetheless. It was a chance to get our fingers in gear, set some levels, get our blood up to operating temperature. We actually spent most of the song turned into each other, away from the audience, talking—yelling really—over the music as we ironed out the kinks of our second-hand instruments and finicky amps. "Is that bass in tune?" "Can we back off on that overhead mic? Maybe take some of the hurt out of those cymbals?" and "Where's the set list? Didn't someone bring it?" No panic here, it's how we did it. It was a matter of running out on stage and dealing with things as they come. Like riding the Baja 500: who knows what's around that corner, or over that rise? It's a stage, it's a path, it was meant that daring people should come this way. Whatever happens, whatever we find there, we will handle it somehow if we keep at least one foot on the throttle. We were almost done with the warm-up when we finally got our rickety-ass shit together. I looked out at the audience.

To my surprise, there were now a dozen or so people on the floor. Some were socializing; some were drinking. I saw one or two joints being passed between friends. Everyone was in a clump in the middle of the floor. When the music stopped, the tiny crowd of faces turned to look at the stage. We looked back at them. I shaded my eyes from the bright light, so I could see a bit more detail. Suddenly, a head appeared to rise out of the center of our audience, continuing until I could make out shoulders, and a purple jacket. It was the smallish human, and they were now standing on their chair. I saw them raise their hands, just clear of the others on the floor, and then begin clapping. A person a few feet away started doing it, too, and then another. Someone in the front set their beer on the floor to free their hands, and shouted as they clapped, "Viva la banda! What do we call you?" The rest of them gave a little cheer at this point, and our drummer (quicker than me at reading the room) began clicking off the next song.

We played, we yelled back and forth to decide what to play, we winged it, and we loved every minute. As we played, more people started to trickle into the room. I wasn't sure where they were coming from, as so many had left after Black Heart had finished. We didn't have time to worry about that, though. The room was heating up, people were dancing now, and there was a line at the bar. It stayed that way for another hour, and we held our ground like the mast of a tiny ship under a giant wind. We were propelled by the fire of our newfound fans, rocket-powered under the lights of a stage we had thought would only shed us like water on wax. Yet we were alive, and so was the room.

I turned to the band members, pretending to have a jamfest: air guitar against lead and bass. In reality, I was calling to them, asking them what we were going to do next. We were out of songs, this was it. We had already segued right into the tune we had hoped to use as a curtain call, there was nowhere to go. "We can't stop!" "Just keep playing" and "Make something up!" These were the opinions of the band. That meant I, supposed leader, front-person, centerpiece of this rare holiday feast, had to follow along.

So, we did it. We just played, we made stuff up, we didn't stop. We recycled a couple of previous songs, but we added new twists, new turns. There was no denying the energy, the force that drove the party to a furious scramble of love and angst, pain and relief, boiling blood, evaporated tears. It was draining the angers, worries and regrets of the world into a giant pool in the dance floor, to be trampled into dust by the fanatical revelers that now packed the room.

The smallish human had worked their way to the front, dancing at the edge of the stage. They wore white hair with black streaks, and a purple jacket that flapped open with their movements. I saw writing on the T-shirt beneath, which had not registered until now. As best I could tell in that glance it said, "Leave 'em wanting more!" I saw right then what I had to do.

Turning back to the band, I signaled end-of-song. They all nodded and started to wrap it up. We drew out the ending, all eyes on my upstretched arms. Then, with a jump and a downward sweep like an axe severing the head of a dangerous snake, I closed the song, jumped up to the mic, and yelled, "Thanks everybody, and GOOD NIGHT!!!"

The smallish human stood clapping, directly in front of me, the rest of the audience radiating out behind, like the tail feathers of a giant bird fanned out to fill the shape of the amphitheater. The applause shook the room, holding steady for a few moments. We bowed, curtsied, and waved, wearing our astonished smiles with a growing sense of success. We set our instruments down, and grabbed our water bottles. The applause died down, and much of the crowd started to turn to the door. Those in front stayed. I leaned down and spoke to the smallish human only a few feet away. "You were a real inspiration tonight," I said. "It was like you started the fire, and everything just took off. What's your name?"

"Rose!" They were grinning.

It was difficult to hear in the room, "Rose?" I asked. Then, chuckling, "Like the flower?" Right away I felt a twinge of fear that I might have offended them, but they giggled.

"Sometimes!" Pause, "Then sometimes like a thorn!" They smiled broadly.

I started laughing again, and turned to the band, "Hey. Come meet our biggest fan!"

The band stepped up, but as I turned back to the crowd, Rose was gone. I looked down both ways and into the crowd. Nothing. Not there.

At that point, Ron the stage manager approached us from the wing at stage right. I thought we'd be in trouble for running too long, but he was grinning.

Away from the mic, he spoke to all of us. "You guys," he paused, looking directly at the band for once. He started again, "You folks caused a bit of commotion on the street!" Our confusion must have been obvious, so he continued. "Seriously. The crowd was mostly outside. Then you started getting loud. They all wanted to come back in!" Ron was laughing now. "I had to go out and tell the bouncers to forget the 'no re-entry' rule and open the doors wide!"

I was still processing this when he turned to address the audience. "Let's hear it for..." back to me, using an undertone, "what's your name again?"

I joined him and leaned partway into the mic. "Thorn!" I tossed the word in the air, letting it find its way around the room. I was looking at Ron.

Ron lowered his voice again and cupped his hand over the mic. He looked at me like he was disappointed. "Just 'Thorn'? Like, that's it?"

I wasn't paying attention to Ron, though. I had turned to the crowd, my eyes scanning for our new fan. I leaned in again.

"Rose...?" I called into the mic, hoping to get a response.

Ron angled around the mic to look at me, his face forming a question.

I dipped my head slightly and pointed toward the crowd. "Purple jacket…" I trailed off, but by then Ron was cutting in on me, impatiently shaking his head.

"One more time!" He shouted into the mic now. With a giant grin, waving his arms, he improvised a random band name. "Let's hear it for Rose of a Purple Thorn!"

He turned away, walking off without another glance. I looked at the band. They were all laughing, giving thumbs up.

On the floor there was cheering, applause, and I think some stomping of feet. We lined up and took another bow. Some of us curtsied, and we all blew kisses to the crowd. I swear I could feel Rose watching us, from somewhere out there. The house lights were turned up all the way now, but the cans on the stage still washed us with color, flowing around us, like we stood in a glowing pool of polished tabletop. We were no longer water; we were the wax itself. I felt like there was no going back from here, that our identity as a band had reinvented itself. And, with absolute certainty, I knew these people would be back to see Rose of a Purple Thorn.

Lagrange

The cruise ship was in port, and Rowan could see it from the shuttle. Well, not the ship itself, but the port. Like a signaling mirror, the shiny dish of the giant solar array was a flash in the blackness, almost eighty thousand miles away. It looked like the silvery blue fireball of a magnesium torch, constantly sinking in the endless sea of space. The ship waited somewhere in the middle of that distant edifice. Hamsa was watching it, too, from the cabin window, until the glimmer of the port disappeared behind the moon.

This was the vacation they had been dreaming of for forever. The idea had come up shortly after they'd started dating, although not seriously at first. However, as conversations kept bringing the subject around, eventually the idea became a dream. As soon as they moved in together, they began putting away money for this adventure. For a while, they agreed they would either take the cruise or spend the money on "something fun," if the expensive vacation proved out of reach. But their fortunes held, the couple saved carefully, the dream became a plan, and here they were.

"Did you remember that thing you forgot?" asked Rowan.

Hamsa winced, startled. "What thing?"

"I don't know. There's always something. Hopefully, you remembered!"

A quick smirk. "I'm pretty sure I remembered everything. And if not, I'll just have to face the punishment of overpaying for it on board!"

The first stop was Libra Station, with its constant stream of shuttles carrying earthlings and cargo to and from the surface, to be sorted and loaded onto the big logistics ships bound for the outer-orbit facilities. Rowan watched the tray-table display, currently showing the Libra approach. In the horizontal screen, it looked like the station was drawing near the shuttle, from below, like a whale surfacing from under a boat. "It's coming right at us!" Rowan exclaimed in mock horror, causing Hamsa to turn from the newsreader.

Hamsa looked at the display, gave a whispered scream, "Ahhhh!" then added, "It really does look like it." They both chuckled.

Hamsa had been to Libra Station quite a bit for work. Rowan, experiencing this for the first time, was in awe of the stark beauty of the surroundings, and filled with admiration for the engineers who conceived of such a place. Libra was situated at L1, the exact point between Moon and Earth where the forces of the two gravity fields came into balance. Rowan envisioned the station as a large, flat rock in the middle of a stream; dark, clear currents from two gravity wells flowing around it, with the shuttle simply making a hop from the shore. In this orbit, the first "Lagrange" point, the facility could maintain its position with a very low energy cost, to serve as a stepping stone, playing leapfrog with the Moon on the way to the port at L2.

After decompressing and decontamination, the couple, each in turn, floated barefoot through the TSA scanner. Rowan was struggling to get the magnetic shoes back on, an oddly difficult task in zero-g. It felt awkward doing it in front of Hamsa, and the situation only got worse as Rowan began to drift away from the bench. Fortunately, the more experienced partner already had the shoes on, and managed to stand and catch Rowan out of the air. "Great carnival balloon act!" Hamsa was trying not to laugh, but failing. "There's a belt on the bench, it's pretty handy until the shoes are on."

Rowan felt a rising flush, "You might have said…"

"Hey, I didn't know about the strap until my about my fifth trip!" Grinning, "It's freefall initiation; everyone has to bounce off the ceiling once or twice to entertain the regulars. It's a thing."

By now, they were both standing upright again. Rowan was about to make a snarky reply but was startled by the interruption of a woman's voice.

"Excuse me," the angular features of the dark-haired security agent were stern but impassive, "Is that your bag?" she was gesturing toward the inspection area. Two more agents, arms folded across their chests, stood rigidly next to a carry-on which lay open, a few feet past the baggage scanner. Nearby travelers were already starting to stare, probably worried that a security incident would slow down the checkpoint and inconvenience them.

Rowan remained casual. "Yes. Is there a problem?"

"I'm going to have to ask you to step over there." Pointing first to the inspection area, then at Hamsa. "Is this your spouse? They'll need to come too."

Rowan let out an involuntary giggle and began to follow. "We're not married—just a special someone."

The agent remained poker-faced and, pointing, herded the couple past the roped-off queue to the inspection area. Another agent held up a see-through evidence bag containing a small object.

"What is this?" he asked, firm and disconnected, like the first agent. "Is it yours?"

"No!" Rowan was flustered. "Well, it looks like my hand sanitizer from home, but I didn't pack it!"

"We've detected a disallowed substance in this container," agent Suwan explained. "We will need to place you in a holding room while we do detailed testing of it as well as the rest of your bags." She was gesturing to another agent to follow, then pointed the direction for Rowan and Hamsa to proceed.

"Wait, Miss…" Rowan looked at the agent's nametag, "Miss Suwan. It's only hand sanitizer! Are we being arrested?"

Hamsa finally seemed to get it together and jumped in. "Where are we going? How long will this take?"

Agent Suwan answered as they all walked down a short hallway. "No," she said. "You will only be in a waiting area while we run our checks. The room is right here." She was gesturing toward a door, which the other agent already held open.

A moment later they were alone, with the door closed, the babble and buzz of the busy TSA checkpoint silenced by the thick walls of the space station. Hamsa whispered, "I have a confession to make."

Rowan had had only a few seconds to take in the details of the room. It appeared to be a small meeting room, with a long table and a few chairs scattered around it. To the right was a large window, filling most of the wall, and another on the left, directly opposite. The glass seemed nearly opaque as it reflected the interior light back into the room. Rowan turned to face Hamsa, who had remained near the door, one hand on the light switch, clearly trying to contain great excitement. Rowan took a slow breath to remain composed.

Hamsa was smiling broadly now. "You know I have friends that work here, right? We're not in trouble, Row. I kinda planned this. Those agents are in on it." After a very short pause, Hamsa's hand flicked the switch, turning off the lights.

Immediately, the starry blackness of space became visible through the two large windows, and the room was filled with a low glow from the two celestial bodies that were strikingly prominent in the frames. Rowan gasped, walked further into the room, and slowly sat down on the edge of the table. To the left was the Moon, half full, bright, in bold relief, and many times the size one would normally see it from Earth. And then, in the opposite window, there was Earth itself. It was clear and blue, in the same phase as the moon, with Africa visible in the sunlit half. Hamsa joined the table-seat.

There were no words. The couple simply sat, looking left, then right, and back again. There was no sound here but the lover's quiet breaths. Perhaps, at the edges of perception, their low heartbeats skipped in the sand, to the imaginary rush of seashells on a calm beach, or swam with spring breezes among fields of vibrant blooms. The light from the Earth and the Moon lapped at the feet of their souls, like cool waters on the shores of some endless river, slowly winding its way through untouched forests of distant time.

It was Rowan who broke the silence. "They're the same size." It was no more than a whisper. "From this spot, they're equal."

Hamsa responded in a dreamish voice. "Libra is at L1, the balance between the two bodies."

"Yeah." Rowan was nodding. "There's nowhere else you could see it like this."

"Very true, and not even on Libra itself. There is no other place on the entire station with windows on both sides like this—just this one meeting room. It's the only place in the universe with this particular view."

After a pause, Rowan said, "What an amazing place to stop as we set out on the cruise."

"Row," Hamsa began, shifting so as to better face each other, "I got us in here for a reason…" An outstretched hand was holding a small box.

Rowan, only mildly surprised, had been waiting for this moment to come. "Hamsa," soft, clear, "Are you going to ask me to marry you?"

Hamsa was somewhat taken aback. "Well, I… yes?" It sounded like a question.

Rowan giggled, "Are you asking me if you were about to ask me to marry you?"

Now Hamsa was beginning to blush. "No, not asking, I mean, I'm asking…"

Rowan could not resist laughing out loud at this point. "Okay, Ham, do you want to walk out to the hall, collect yourself, then come in and try again?"

Hamsa thought for a minute. The mood was light, the confusion was a bit funny, but this should be a solemn moment. "Yes," nodding, "Yes, I do. I'll be right back."

Rowan sat in the darkened room, looking out the two windows. The Earth, the Moon, caressing each other in the embrace of invisible arms, billions of years together, eons circling each other. "You shall be together when the white wings of death scatter you." The poem surfaced from memory, and Rowan whispered it to the empty room. "Yes, you shall be together even in the silent memory of God. But let there be space in your togetherness, and let the winds of the heavens dance between you."

There was a knock at the door. Rowan crossed the room and casually opened it.

Hamsa stood there, sheepishly grimacing. "Sorry, I couldn't open the door—no security card."

"This just keeps getting better, Ham!"

But instead of laughing, the lovers just smiled as Hamsa held up the box, opened it to reveal the ring—sparkling symbol of eternity—a golden rope with a diamond knot, the circle, the cycle, the orbital path. Hamsa asked simply, "Will you?"

Rowan examined the ring, smiled broadly without saying a word, then slid one hand into a coat pocket, retrieving a small box. Hamsa stared at the box a moment, then up at Rowan's face. They started to laugh and placed the boxes side by side on the table, both lids open.

"Did you know?" Hamsa asked.

Rowan gave a little snort. "Nope." Pause. "I mean, I thought you might do it sometime soon, maybe even during the cruise. I was going to pop the question on day one, so I could beat you to it!"

"But you had the ring in your pocket right now?"

"I didn't want to trust it with my baggage. Besides, you never know when the moment might seem right."

Hamsa sighed, "Yes."

"Is that your final answer?" This got a giggle.

"Yes, under one condition."

Rowan raised an eyebrow. "Oh? And what is that?"

"You probably shouldn't call me 'Ham.'"

Rowan looked confused.

"I'm Muslim," Hamsa explained, "I don't really care, but I think my parents would be offended."

They both laughed a bit at the thought. It settled down quickly, followed by a short pause as they gazed out the windows.

"Yes."

"Yes."

They continued to watch the Earth and Moon, to the silent applause of surrounding stars. This was a moment that would never come back, in a place that most people would never see, and neither of them wanted it to end. The rings had been sitting on the table the whole time, as if waiting for their part in this ritual, but the couple only leaned on each other, fingers interlaced in their shared lap, imagining a new future they had already started.

Eventually, they turned, made eye contact, and then stood, stretching luxuriously. They retrieved the rings, removed them from the boxes, and each presented their left hand to the other.

As the rings slid into place, the lovers met each other's gaze, "Stand together but not too near together," Hamsa quoted, in a makeshift ceremony. "For the pillars of the temple stand apart."

Rowan smiled, saying, "And the oak tree and the cypress grow not in each other's shadow."

Up Draught Coffee Co

Wednesday Morning

Jill and Indy were by the rail today, a table for two, near the flower beds along the sidewalk. They could overhear the conversations of a few pedestrians that came breezing by, oblivious to the café patrons that were literally within arm's reach. Snippets of small talk, mostly, with occasional scraps that yanked on Indy's curiosity strings.

"…Knew what was going to happen to that stock. Haven't you been watching the market? You should…." Then they were out of earshot. What stock? What should they do? Buy? Sell?

"I'm going back to Oklahoma. I don't have a choice!" This person sounded agitated. Indy wondered, no choice, really? Or, refusing to choose?

"Is she fucking him? Because that makes a difference…" Of course it makes a difference! But how did we get to that part of the conversation in the first place?

Then there was that woman who walked briskly, in stiff silence. She stood out somehow, like a barely audible scream from a dark alley. "There's something I need to say to her," Indy thought, "I just don't know what…"

The parade of passersby continued, one mysterious traveler after another, all of them unwittingly panhandling for questions. Indy's speculation was interrupted by Jill.

"Hey…?" she had leaned across the table, waving her hands in front of Indy's face, "Looks like the lights are on—anybody home?"

"Huh?" quickly assessing the surroundings, coming in for a landing, "Oh. Sorry! I was distracted by the people walking by. By their talking…"

"You were eavesdropping?" Jill snickered her disapproval. "Can you take off your conversation-burglar ski mask and hang out with me?"

Indy flushed briefly, looking around to latch onto something else, something to dodge with. "I've never understood the name of this place."

"Why?" Jill raised her eyebrows. "The double entendre, 'Up Draught Coffee Company'?"

"Wait," Indy was mildly shocked, "I've been coming here for, like, a year since it changed, and never heard anyone pronounce the name? I mean, we all just call it 'the café.' I've been reading the sign as 'Up Drought' this whole time!"

Jill was laughing hard, now. "You're the word boi, Indy! You should know it sounds like 'draft' when you read it!" She had to take a breath, then resumed conversational tone. "That's the point: 'up draft,' like a kind of breeze, but 'draught,' as in pouring liquid." A slight chuckle at the end.

Indy was now wearing an unmistakable stare of epiphany. "So, the tagline," pointing at the window art, "saying, 'Words on Tap'… that builds on it!"

Now Jill was the surprised one. "Okay, I actually didn't make that connection! But yeah, the open mic, the story slam, that makes sense."

"And writers' blog." Indy was smiling. "The stuff they have online—local writers, recordings of the story events, I've even got some poetry there—I've always seen that part as the meaning of 'on tap,' like the sign says." Pause. "I just never noticed the name says 'draught,' and not 'drought'!

"That's what you have me for!" Jill smiled.

"True, you catch me when I'm being dense." Grin. "You've been doing it most of my life! We've been friends for what, fifteen years?"

"I was best woman at your wedding. That was ten years ago. How long had I known you before that?"

"Ah, yes." Indy's brow wrinkled for a moment, recalling freshman year of high school before continuing, "So, twenty, then. I'm older than I think."

She suddenly veered, "And you still can't read me."

Indy felt a tinge of annoyance, it faded quickly. "Uh... did I miss something?" He looked at Jill's face for a moment, then continued, "I did notice you seemed a little dejected. I just figured it was a rough week at school."

"Your woman's intuition is slacking, but only a little." Jill took a breath, releasing it in a slow sigh, while Indy waited. "Today is my mother's birthday." She had developed a distant look. "I've been thinking about her a lot."

"Oh." For once, Indy was at a loss for words. The sunlit scene had suddenly become a bit chilly and Indy felt that a sweater would be comforting right about now.

"I'll graduate this spring." Jill's voice had become husky. "The first in my family to finish college, much less grad school. I wish she could see it."

"She'd be proud of you."

"Do you know that she dropped out of Purdue to become a housewife?"

"She would be really, really proud of you."

"Indy," Jill appeared to be both sad and appreciative at the same time. "I'm so grateful for you. I don't usually hang out with women unless I'm dating them, and men always seem to want something from me. You're one of the few humans I'm actually comfortable with."

Indy smiled, nodding. It wasn't the first time Jill and he had had this conversation. He replied in kind. "And women always seem to want me around," he said, "once they feel my affinity for them. Sometimes it's overwhelming, picking up their emotions. You're on a different channel. I don't read you unless I choose to listen."

Jill smiled. "At least you do listen sometimes."

"I love you." Indy said, in clear, platonic meter. "And I know your mom did, too. So much so that she must have known you would reach this place. She knew that someday you would rise above your childhood expectations, become the woman she could not." Indy was looking directly into Jill's eyes, two souls briefly touching fingertips. "You are that woman."

Jill's eyes were damp. She swallowed, sniffled slightly, and sighed. "That's what I'm talking about," she said. "You're a good listener."

Friday Night

The lights were low. Just so, like a room full of electric candles. Up Draught Coffee Company was packed, while the street was an empty river of feathery mist. Out there, the evening was over. But inside, things were just warming up. Indy and Kasha arrived, found Jill waiting with a couple of friends. There were places for them at the table, so they ordered coffee and dessert at the counter, then sat down with the group. The first reader had just finished, the host was calling a name and reminding poets to get on the list. "If you want to 'dare' your work with the crowd," they said.

"Sharing is daring!" Sozz was a bundle of encouragement, always available to feed enthusiasm to nervous performers of any stripe. "Did you put your name down?" Indy started to get back up, with a sheepish grin.

"I did it, Hon." Kasha was grinning. "I didn't want to miss out on your latest work!"

Another reader was up, shuffling papers in mock confusion to lighten the mood before he shared. His work, when he began, was lilting and fluid, a worthy delivery, and the verse was delightful.

"He's good," Indy remarked.

"Yeah," it was Kasha, "Still waiting for you to come up." She smiled, leaning into Indy a little more.

Coffee arrived at the table a few minutes later, followed almost immediately by a new face, an attractive young woman who seemed to have her eye on Jill. Jill immediately waved the newcomer over to the one remaining seat.

"Everyone," Jill raised her voice just enough to be heard, trying not to disturb the current reader, "Meet Cammie." She gestured. "Cammie, meet everyone." She proceeded to point to each in turn, "This is Kasha and her husband, Indy, then Sozz, and this one is Claire," Jill slipped her arm around Claire as she said her name, making a coy smile, then adding, "she's with me."

"Hi!" Five voices, nearly unison.

Cammie sat. Indy watched her face for few seconds, then looked away. There was something about her, something intriguing, unusual. He made a mental note to follow up.

"How do you know Jill?" It was Sozz, speaking to Cammie.

"I don't." Cammie said, perfect deadpan. "And actually, my name's Emilie, Jill was just inviting a random stranger to your table."

Most of the table had turned to watch the stage, listening to the reader, but they all looked back at Cammie now, mildly startled.

Sozz was clearly astonished. "Really?"

"No," Cammie smiled, just a tiny bit, "Not really. I know her from Girl Scouts."

This got a chuckle from the table, but Sozz was doubtful. Looking quickly at Jill, who remained poker-faced, Sozz asked again, "Really?"

"No," Cammie's smile was unchanged. "But I got you twice, now."

Indy had been observing this exchange along with everyone else. He laughed with the rest of them, then gave a quizzical shake of his head, and looked back at the stage. Jill was explaining to Sozz that Cammie was a friend from college, from a few years ago, before grad school. She had recently returned to California, and that neither of them had ever, ever been a Girl Scout. Conversation continued between Cammie and Sozz, in short, quiet breaks, trying to avoid stepping on the show. Indy listened to the readers with one ear, picking up the low commentary at the table with the other. She doesn't really talk like a girl, Indy thought to himself, not really. It was an odd moment, but one quickly swept aside in favor of the performance on stage.

The current reader was good. Energetic, bold, flowing and pausing, to eventually arrive at a clear ending that received a decisive round of snaps. The readers always tended to get better as the night wore on, as the crowd woke up to the inspired messages flowing from the makeshift stage in the corner of the ancient, high-ceilinged room. The eclectic décor of the café lent itself well to the open mic, with mid-century modern chairs next to hybrid Queen Annes, bean bags for the psychedelic crowd, and picnic benches along the tapestry-draped walls of the late Victorian shop. The paneling wore the work of numerous local artists, as did most of the ceiling. Even the floor was decorated with a mosaic tile inset, polished beach glass set by students from the satellite campus.

Indy always felt comfortable here, especially when it was full. There were a few regulars, but many new faces as well. There always were. The café was situated at the crossroads between the remote college campus and the old business district, both of which attracted visitors. With a strong art scene, the community was sometimes home to temporary residents—actors, festival performers, musicians—hosted by patrons or fellow artists for the length of their particular program. Then there were the college students. These were the ones who never had any money to spend but could somehow afford endless cappuccinos and expensive pastries. The students were the lifeblood of Up Draught.

Suddenly, the host was back at the mic, calling for Indy. It was time.

Indy stepped up, two sheets of neatly folded, handwritten paper in hand. He stood for a moment, inspecting the crowd.

"I wrote this one yesterday," Indy began, "and I'll admit, I haven't reread it. But I remember liking it then, so let's check it out together, okay?"

The room laughed gently, all eyes on the familiar form of Indy at the mic.

After a throat-clearing cough, Indy began.

The Tomboy

my mother, bless her heart
always dressed me like a boy
I didn't protest, I didn't know how
so, I became a boy for my mother's sake
a tomboy on the loose
it has some rewards
one of the guys, one of the girls
I could be myself, I could be someone else
I wore my boyfriend's flannel
several sizes bigger than me
the loose fabric hanging in folds
concealed the body that was developing
into something I could not inhabit
it made me feel like a girl
sleeves too long
fingertips peeking out
like a ceremonial kimono
I wrote my girlfriend's essay for her
because I was good at it

she would bat her eyelashes at me
and my heart would melt
wearing the hat of some missing hero
how could I resist the wiles of someone
who made me feel so much like a boy
but at the same time
she and I could be the same
a tomboy on the loose
but a thorn in my side
not one of the guys, not one of the girls
can't be myself, can't be someone else

Indy paused at this point, for effect. Then he continued, with heightened voice.

my friends call me "Gabby"
I don't have any friends
my license calls me "Gabe"
I don't have any license

At first, the room was silent. Indy thought he could hear the dripping sound of a bathroom faucet, as if someone hadn't tightened it all the way. A bead of sweat was thinking about forming on his brow. In reality, the pause only stayed around for a few seconds, until a snapping came from the direction of Indy's table. It was Cammie. As soon as she started, the whole room snapped along, a few people clapping as well. It was possibly the loudest applause of the entire night. Indy took a bow, then a curtsy, said "Thank you!" into the mic, and returned to his seat.

Cammie had switched places with Sozz, so Indy now sat between her and Kasha.

"That was one of your best, Indy." Kasha said with an affectionate smile, "Really good."

"I was worried for a sec, with that pause."

"They were probably just blown away."

Cammie jumped in, "Did they already know?" She paused, then winced. "I mean, can I have your pronouns?"

"He's seriously co-dependent," Sozz teased. "His pronouns are 'you' and 'yours'!"

The whole table laughed at this one, with Kasha and Jill both nodding. "Yep!" They said, and "Can confirm!" By now the next reader was starting, taking the focus away from the table.

It was actually two speakers, standing together at the mic. They delivered from memory, starting with the one on the left, alone at first.

Made so plain,
that all feel and understand it,
even down to brutes and creeping insects.
The ant,
who has toiled and dragged a crumb to his nest,
will furiously defend the fruit of his labor,
against whatever robber assails him.

Then, as the first speaker started to repeat this verse, the other leaned in to share the mic. They began deliberately, mashing new words on top of the beautiful verse which was being delivered exactly as before. The effect was discordant, somewhat eerie, and completely unintelligible. Once the conjoined verse completed, speaker one stopped, stepping back from the mic. The second speaker repeated the verse they'd introduced.

Involves the use of force,
fraud, or coercion to obtain

some type of labor or commercial
sex act.
Every year, millions of men, women,
and children are trafficked worldwide
including right here in the United States.

A round of snaps followed. The two readers bowed, then each stepped back to the mic, in turn.

"That," the first one said, "was a bit of Lincoln's 1858 speech on slavery and the American Dream..."

Then the second took over to finish the explanation, "...mixed with the first two sentences on the Department of Homeland Security's webpage on human trafficking."

There was now applause, as the two bowed one more time and left the stage.

"That was crazy good!" Sozz was saying. Jill and Claire excused themselves to go talk to the speakers.

"It was pretty cool," agreed Cammie. "I liked yours better," smiling sweetly. "Also, I still want your pronouns." She was looking at Indy expectantly.

He paused as the host announced the end of the open mic, leading the house in a final show of appreciation. "Sorry, I forgot you'd asked. He, and they."

Sunday Afternoon

The café was mostly empty, but it was nice out, so Indy grabbed an outdoor seat. He began tuning into the pedestrian world, which was sparse but interesting today. Sunday afternoons were inhabited by a different crowd. More visitors, fewer locals, and everyone wore play clothes of one sort or another. Conversations were mostly out of earshot, but Indy found it interesting to take inventory of the passing faces, making guesses as to their personalities, careers, and where they grew up. It was a silly game, but comforting in a childish way. Occasionally, Indy would later find out he was right about someone. It was a little spooky, but probably just a fluke, memory backfill, picking up on subliminal cues, or something else. It was still fun.

Jill arrived, accompanied by Cammie. Once again, Indy was struck by a mildly odd sensation around Jill's old friend. Here was someone he could not read at all, much to his annoyance. They greeted each other, then both disappeared into the café to order. Indy started reflecting on Friday night: the reading, the laughter, the amazing performances, and meeting Cammie. What had she said?

Something about himself. What was it? He ran back through the conversation, searching for the thing. There was a joke, pranking Sozz, right off the bat. There were the spontaneous comments here and there. Cammie was bold, direct, assertive, enough for Indy to be envious of her confidence, at least a little. Then there was the question about his pronouns. Nothing odd about that, really. But the way it sounded—it had a funny ring, especially the second time.

Now the two girls had returned to the table, coffee in hand. "So," Indy began, "Girl Scouts, huh?" Jill looked confused. Cammie was about to laugh when Indy added, "So is that lesbian code for, uh, dating or something?"

Jill remembered Cammie's wisecracks. "Not as far as I know," she said, "and definitely not in this case. Cammie wouldn't take me out, as much as I flirted!"

"Wait," Cammie was acting surprised, "You flirted? I'm so fucking dense!" She laughed, they all did.

Indy was still mulling over his reflections from a few minutes earlier. Something suddenly clicked.

"But you are gay, am I right?" It was a leap, but Indy was suddenly confident in his intuition.

"I'm only into men, really…" Cammie was hesitant, even while protesting. Her demeanor seemed to bear out Indy's theory.

"Yes, but do you really consider yourself a woman?"

Jill was clearly shocked. "Indy," she wasn't angry, and knew him too well to doubt his motivation, but this was new. "What exactly are you saying?"

Cammie intercepted the question. "I think he just figured me out." She snickered, adding, "That's a first!" She was looking at Indy but turned to Jill before continuing. "Yes, Jill, I look like a girl, dress like one, but you know I mainly hang out with men, right? Like, one of the boys?"

Jill was nodding. "Yeah, I kinda knew that… I guess. Never really thought much about it."

"For me, my attraction to men is gay. It's what's inside that matters." She chuckled, "A lot of straight men would be pretty shocked if they could see inside my head… see what I actually look like to myself!"

"And what's that?"

"Basically," Cammie pointed at Indy, "him."

Indy was grinning now. "That's fucking hilarious." He started to laugh, making it hard to continue, "Hang on…"

still laughing. The girls sat there, eyebrows raised, waiting for the punchline. "Okay," Indy was catching his breath. "Okay. I was just thinking, just before you sat down. Two things, really. With Cammie I don't really feel the kind of affinity I usually do for women, so I figured, you know, she wasn't, on some level." He smiled, saw confirmation in Cammie's expression, and continued. "At the same time," he paused, trying not to start laughing again, "Cammie looks strikingly like my own self-image!"

"I knew it!" Cammie was nodding, relieved, amused, satisfied, and obviously on board with this. "Like looking in a mirror, huh?" She was nodding emphatically.

"Exactly."

"You two are fucking weird." Jill was rolling her eyes in mock contempt, while obviously enjoying this moment of bonding revelation between her two good friends. The mood was light, like the Sunday afternoon air itself. From the café one could smell the weekend batch of coffee beans roasting, while the street side was lined with the blooms of hyacinth and white iris, subtle in the soft breeze. An atmosphere of harmony, somehow suited to the matched pair of counterparts sitting to either side of Jill.

"So," Cammie began, "why just 'he/they'? It sounds like you'd qualify for a 'she' at the end…"

Indy would normally be annoyed by this, but Cammie had earned some license. "I might as well just say 'any/any' when people ask." He made a gesture of defeat as he spoke. "Then I would be allowing them to choose my pronouns for me, wouldn't I? I'm not okay with that." He paused, looking at Cammie. "You've not given me yours…."

"She, and they." Cammie dipped in an ironic nod. "Same reason. I can live with 'she,' and it puts me in control."

They sipped coffee for a few moments. Eventually, Jill asked, "Cammie, would you have asked Indy anything, you know, if it weren't for the poem?"

"Probably not." She sat reflecting for a moment, then said, "It was like you wrote it for me."

With no trace of irony, Indy said simply, "I did."

War Trees

Outside was the biting sleet and oppressive gray of the mountains in January, cold and unforgiving. Inside the café it was an oasis. A mock spring, with green ferns in the corners, orchids on the counter, colorful artwork hanging from tall Victorian walls, and colored lights remaining from Christmas of two years past. Indy usually found these things were enough to cheer him up, but not today.

A bright collection of flowered teapots and mismatched cups rested in a farmhouse hutch, with a small sign reading "for display only," although several of the guests were using them. Regulars, of course. If anyone but a local were to open the hutch, they would probably be asked politely not to touch the antiques. Indy grabbed his favorite pot and took it to the counter for tea. The barista was uncharacteristically subdued. The headlines could be seen on his face, too, like a bold Sharpie on white cardboard.

Indy balanced his teapot, cup, and pastry carefully as he walked to his favorite table. The crumbs of ice in the freezing rain were visibly accumulating along the bottom edge of the casement windows, in severe contrast to the dancing flamelights of the fake fireplace only an arm's length away. The thin pane of glass, an invisible shield separating the harsh environment from the temperate hospitality of the café. Indy shivered involuntarily with a wave of... what? Sadness? Remorse? Anger? Fear? Angst? Or resignation, maybe? The loss of a great leader, the shattering of the glass that had kept the hostile elements at bay.

It was a day to mourn. Mostly alone, but with the company of the characters in the book Indy now held close to his face. Nothing else was working, so escape was the only option. Devouring the story with a side of tea, the room began to fade, and the low buzz of the coffee shop became background tones for the scenes on the pages. The occasional interruptions—a smile and wave to a friend and pouring another cup of tea—became fewer and further between, as Indy found the desired level of deep solace through isolation. Today's grief began to distance itself. Like a jackal, eventually wandering away from a stubbornly treed cat. Indy was vaguely aware of a person sliding into the adjacent chair, and did not raise his eyes.

"You know how sometimes, in a grove of oak trees," Cammie began as though they had already been chatting, "sometimes there are little groups of smaller oaks clumped together?" Indy peered over the top of his book. He realized he'd been isolating for quite a while, so he dog-eared the page and set the whole thing down on the table.

"Good morning, Cammie!"

She ignored the greeting, continuing her line of thought. "I mean," she said, "there might be lots of giant oaks in the grove. Big ones, what would take two or three people to touch hands around the trunk. But then every so often you will find a clump of smaller ones, and these will always be arranged in a ring. You know what I'm talking about?" Indy wasn't sure, but nodded, to play along. Cammie continued, "This happens when one of the big trees has been cut down. Fifty years ago, or maybe a hundred. Just long enough for some branches to form around the stump, and those branches to eventually grow into trees. That's why they form little rings. The stump may be long gone now, leaving only a little circle of sister oaks."

Indy realized that there were trees like this down by the river. He'd seen some of them there. "Yes," thoughtfully, "that makes sense."

Cammie continued, "Sometimes, you will see a forest composed only of these tree rings. Ring after ring, easily mistaken for separate trunks, but all really growing from old stumps. A forest like that would have been, at some time in the past, completely razed. Perhaps clear-cut during the Gold Rush. Whole hillsides of nothing but stumps." Cammie paused, and added, "But now there are how many trees? Three, or even four of them for every one that was cut? Like a slow-motion hydra, over hundreds of years, many lifetimes, the forest multiplies in the face of injury."

"Did you just read that?" Indy was looking at the stack of books on the table, trying to see which it might have come from.

"No," Cammie said. "I don't really know where that came from. It sounds like the kind of thing my dad would have told me, but I don't recall him saying it." There was a contemplative pause. "I think of it now, because it describes martyrdom, in a way. If the tree had lived, it would have grown old, and eventually fallen over. However, by being cut down, its power is multiplied."

Indy stared blankly, as though the room was on fire but no one else was noticing it. "You're telling me that

Ren's death will be worth it," he said. "Is that what you mean?"

"No." Cammie was shaking her head emphatically. "Ren is more powerful now that they are gone than they were when they carried the torch for us. The news has been blasted across the countryside, and the whole world knows about Ren. The cause has been picked up by a mob of angry people who will storm the castle in Ren's name. The movement will probably make a difference. In fact, this generation of activists will likely change everything. But, no, it's not 'worth it,' in terms of the exchange. It isn't, in the same way that the little rings of oaks have not replaced the groves. The old forest is gone; it is not coming back. The new forest remains to be seen. It's different. It's unstoppable. It's a miracle. It's a radical evolution, and an overwhelming wave of progress. It's many things, but there is no worth here, not in the conflict itself." Cammie paused, nearly out of breath. "There is no trade off. More trees do not make more value. The river only flows one way."

Indy looked at Cammie's face for a moment, then responded, "I think you're ready for open mic night."

Cammie just laughed. "You're the writer," she said.

"I'm reminded of a poet who said, 'It's not the shadow, it's the light that casts it,' or something to that effect."

"Sounds familiar."

Indy took a sip of tea, now quite cold cold from neglect. He looked out of the window for a long minute.

Cammie broke in. "Good Afternoon, by the way."

"What...?"

"You said 'Good Morning.' It's mid-afternoon." She paused. "I came to get you."

"Oh." Indy remained thoughtful. "We have stuff to do, don't we?" It was not really a question. "I guess we'd better get busy."

The icy rain was starting to become snow, but the sky seemed a little brighter than it had this morning. Cammie followed Indy as he carried his dishes to the counter, where they both ordered coffee to go. Retrieving coats from the mirrored hall-tree, they scrambled into them, slipped into their gloves, pulled hoods up. Cammie held the door open for Indy as they set out to battle the elements.

At Water's Edge

I stopped just short of the water's edge. I hadn't expected this situation at all, as the trail was well-worn, and seemed like it should continue. There were even stepping stones, here in the muddy part of the path, poached from the nearby land and placed by some anonymous traveler, apparently for the benefit of anyone who would find them later. There was no sign posted, no warning whatsoever. Yet there it was: a pond, directly in the way. I looked left, and I looked right, but there were no signs of travel in either direction along the shore. One minute I was strolling along the path, the next my progress was cut short. The pond itself was not newly flooded, but old, and well-established, its marshy clumps of reeds overhanging the sandy earth of the shoreline. The trail just seemed to end here, as though it were the final destination.

I was perplexed. I craned my neck, seeking any sign that there might be others in the area. No one. I was alone. Did people come here to wash things like clothing, or to bathe? That would explain the need for such a path. But there were no real signs of activity here, the trail simply ended at the water's edge. Did people come here to fish? No way to be sure, but there were no obvious signs of fishing, and no dock, no fishing boats. Did people come here to gather water then? Possibly. The pond seemed clear, and fresh, as though it were fed by unseen springs. Cool water, rising from the depths of the rocks deep in the earth beneath my feet. It was a thought that felt refreshing, soothing, and reminding me that my feet were tired. I looked around for a clear space to rest on the low grass beside the trail.

Perhaps this is what people do here, I thought to myself. Perhaps they come to relax, and spend a few hours or minutes in the light of the late sun. To inhale the smell of the mud at the water's edge; to listen and hear the small sounds of insects about their insect business and the talking breezes which chattered in a language of near understanding. Perhaps people come here simply to marvel at the tiny waves lapping the shore, whose miniature tongues curl like so many flames, persistently seeking to move, and then to re-move, the division between water and earth. This was a musical place, with rhythm, and harmony.

I may have fallen asleep for a while, but the sun had only advanced by the smallest degree. Time seemed to scrape its belly on the trail before the water's edge, hanging low on its tired legs, as though urging me to continue alone. It was a lazy kind of day anyway, in late fall, with its blend of warm sun and chill drafts of air. The kind of day in which anything could happen, but nothing actually did. I would like to go on record to say that I believe in nothing beyond the present, as the future is unseen, will always be unseen, and each moment slips into the past before we can even put our arms around it. Why should this philosophical ditty matter now? Does it need to matter?

I looked back down the trail which led me to this spot. It was long and meandering. Sometimes steep, sometimes slick with moss, sometimes rocky, with sharp, dangerous edges, while on other days totally unremarkable, tame, even seductive. I don't know what I expected to find, when I began this path, but this place was a surprise. I should say, "is" a surprise, as there is only this moment, the present—only now. This is a surprise. The trail is long. The water is clear, and calm, and settling into the nest of its vale like a cat settles in the laundry basket.

I am looking out to the lake now. It is bigger than I had thought, and I now see that it is dotted with small islands. I see trees on some of the islands, shrouded in a light mist, and having a bit of glow about them as the sunset places the leafless branches in soft silhouette. In my mind's eye, I can see movement on the islands, but I know this is whimsy, or the work of an overactive imagination. I can feel that this place is only for me, and the otherworldly shadows that leap from island to island are just that—shadows, of another life, or another place, not really part of this landscape. I'm fairly certain this is not a dream, but I begin to wonder if I am awake.

I am standing beside my father now, as he was when I was small. He is supine on the lawn. I leap upon him, but he catches me and holds me at arm's length over his head. He lowers his arms, then pushes me back up, and I feel myself fall, bouncing on his chest as he laughs. I can feel that he is solid, immovable, permanent. Now I stand beside his bed as he becomes part of the world that gave him to me, fading into the rocks, the forest wood, the ocean—solid, immovable, permanent.

I walk now with my mother, and hold her hand. I can smell her perfume, and the hand lotion on her fingers, now on my fingers. Her lips are moving, but her words are so quiet, fading to pastel, then watercolor, now an unfinished veil painting, with no firm designs, no edges. I have so many questions for her, but each moment slips into the past before we can even put our arms around it. I know the answers, to be sure, but to hear them in her voice: I would walk back down this trail a thousand times over.

At the water's edge, I examine myself in the liquid mirror. I see my father's chin, my mother's eyes, my sister's ambition, my brother's memory. I see the hopes and dreams of my children, the lines and creases of past loves, together, in the present, right now. They are all in the face looking up from the water, but through them I see something new, something I hadn't noticed before. Something in the water itself.

I have been standing at the water's edge, letting so many moments sift through my fingers, like bits of grain in a sieve, or the raindrops that had begun to obliterate the trail at my back, and I had not noticed something behind my own reflection. The glassy surface of the lake reveals its secrets as the sun begins to set, as the reflection gives way to the truth. And looking through my face, I see stones. Stepping stones—and the trail—continuing along, unending, uninterrupted, beneath the vast expanse of water. The shore is only a change in state, not the end.

I laugh as I kick off my shoes. Looking ahead, I continue to follow the trail, the cool liquid lapping about my ankles, my knees, my thighs. The stepping stones have not deserted me, they welcome and become my stride. And now the moment at water's edge has gone, slipping away as all moments do.

The Dreams of the White Farmhouse

There was no sound. Or perhaps there was. Maybe it was something like the ringing of a wine glass, humming with the stroke of a damp finger on its rim, but very, very quiet. No, there was no sound. There was just the green field, stretching to the horizon, the clear blue sky beyond broken only by the ominous advent of the house. It looked sad, alone, and uninhabitable. A white box under a featureless red roof. The stark walls wore curtainless windows, empty black eyes that surveyed the surrounding rows of unknowable carrots, lettuce, or beets. Staring at the house, one could feel its pull, as though it was calling out in the voices of small creatures that crawled and bit in the night, hiding in the attic by day, only to be heard by the doomed and the terminally ill.

Avery woke up to a clammy sweat, the dream of the farmhouse echoed in their head. There was a moment of confusion, looking around the room, trying to identify surroundings, and the sleeping stranger in the bed. In a flash, they recognized their partner Sage, the familiar bed and the room. All confusion evaporated. The alarm clock would sound in less than an hour, there was no use staying in bed at this point. Coffee was in order, after a shower to wash sleepy eyes into focus. The usual enthusiasm began to fill Avery's thoughts, the dream was quickly forgotten.

* * *

Randall reviewed the logs one last time before deleting them. Folders of patient records, neat brown stacks in an otherwise shabby office, stood waiting for service. He paused a moment, looked at the screen, then back at the paper document that faced him from the open folder on the desk. Randall's brow wrinkled a touch in cloudy contemplation. He withdrew his hand from the keyboard, folded his arms across his chest. "Hmm," he sighed, staring at the column of arcane numbers. "Fuck." He closed the folder, placed a blank sticky note on the front, and moved it to one side.

* * *

There was no sound. Wait. A dull roar could be heard off in the distance, an ocean's footsteps stomping some rocky shore into sand. Or it was a breeze: a cold, winter wind whispering through the stick figures of unseen trees just beyond the flat horizon. The house was too far away to see details, but Avery imagined a chimney, cold and dark, like the fireless hearth beneath the red, blood-soaked roof. Waking with a start, they leapt from the bed to look in the mirror, expecting to see a gaunt, mummified face, with yellow teeth grinning below dark sockets of eyes and nostrils.

By the time Avery reached the bathroom, the dream had completely fallen away, the panic that fed on a half-alert mindset failing to survive in the fully awake brain, leaving only a bit of wry laughter in its wake. Avery checked the clock even as Sage stirred, asking, "What time is it?" in a pillow-muffled voice.

"It's early," they answered, "but not too early for me." Avery leaned down, kissing Sage's ear before gathering some clothes and leaving the bedroom.

* * *

Randall held the folder out to Dr. Sondra, who accepted it casually, noticing the sticky. "Something wrong?" she asked, taking a sip of coffee before leaning back a bit in her large, overstuffed office chair.

"There's an anomaly in the numbers." He put his hands on his hips as the doctor opened the folder. "I was looking at the logs from the machine. The series dips for several seconds. It's right before I loaded the program." Randall paused, then added, "I've never seen anything like it."

Dr. Sondra looked thoughtful. "A dip, you say?" She leaned forward, opening the folder.

"Yes." Randall remained at attention.

"Okay." She was silent for a few seconds as she reviewed a few sheets, then she looked up again, and said, "Well, it looks like this one is coming back pretty soon for delivery." She pursed her lips. "Tell Laverne to keep a watch." She handed the folder back with a dismissive glance at Randall.

* * *

The sound was like a buzzing of bees, but also not. It was coming directly from the house, from the glowing white walls, plastered with the chalky paste of wine-soaked flour, ash, and bone meal. The noise was distinct, rolling along the porch and out into the green farmland, turning the scene gray with dead leaves on dying plants, spreading its deadly vibrations. The dark windows revealed shadowy shapes, dancing, flitting from room to room in the awful, profane house. Avery could imagine a basement, dark, odious, filled with crawling worms and maggots, whose eyeless faces wore expressionless grins of bitter hatred and profound despair.

Avery woke suddenly, fully alert in an instant. "This needs to stop."

Sage rolled over, horizontally facing Avery in the dim light. "Another dream?"

"Yeah."

"This has been going on for, like, a week now?"

Avery sat up and stretched. "Yeah," yawning. "I guess. About that, maybe more."

"Maybe you need some edibles."

They laughed, "Maybe. Not sure those last all night, though!"

"You just need some wicked edibles!"

Avery left the bed, giving Sage an affectionate pat on the head. "You're cute," they said, "don't ever change."

Sage smiled, pulled the covers in just a little bit, and called, "Don't forget your appointment." Blank stare from Avery. "Your glasses...?"

"Ah, right."

* * *

Avery was looking forward to the new frames, perhaps more than the new prescription. Sitting in the chair before the concave mirror, they chatted with the optician, who was looking carefully at the alignment as she reached around the mirror, sliding the new glasses into place. "Yeah," Avery smiled. "These are going to rock our wedding pictures!"

"You're getting married?"

"Yes! Sage and I, in just a few weeks."

"Nice!" The optician said, removing the glasses again, making a small adjustment. She handed them back. "Try this."

Avery put on the glasses, looking in the mirror for confirmation, tilting their head slightly side to side.

The optician had the patient file open, a brown folder with a blank sticky note on the cover. She was writing on the delivery form. "Are you ready for your big day?"

"Everything's in order at this point. Now if I could only get a full night's sleep beforehand, that would be great." Avery did an eye-roll and smirked.

The optometrist was impassive. "Trouble sleeping?" She asked?

"Yeah, weird dreams."

"Oh?" a touch of concern. "What sort of dreams?" She looked up.

"A recurring nightmare, really," Avery was still looking in the mirror. The optician watched intently. "There's a white house in a green field, weird sound. It's super spooky, but I don't know why." Avery paused. "I don't remember much details. Just the house, red roof, blue sky. It wakes me up pretty much every night."

"Huh." The optician set the file down on the table. "If you want a little unsolicited advice," her tone was oddly serious, "you shouldn't talk about it." Then added, with emphasis, "To anyone." Avery was a little surprised but listened in silence as the woman continued. "Sometimes dreams freak people out. But they don't mean anything, you know? No reason to get other people worried about your dream, right?"

"Right." Avery swallowed, suppressing a shiver. It was suddenly chilly in the office. "Sure."

The optician smiled. "Great!" She glanced at the chart one more time, made a couple of marks on the page, then closed it, saying, "You're good to go! If you notice any problem when you leave, give me a call." She slid a card over to Avery.

"Okay," reading the card, "Laverne?"

"Yep." Laverne seemed upbeat now. "That's me!"

* * *

"She's having dreams." Randall was saying, "The entry page—she remembers the white house."

Dr. Sondra was mildly concerned. "We've seen this before. Patients dismiss the entry page. They think it's part of the eye test."

"But the numbers in the logs…" Randall was uneasy, speaking quickly in a low voice, "That's not normal. This one has an odd brain pattern. Probably some unusual form of neurodivergence or something."

"Did the program load?"

"I don't think so, I don't know, maybe? If it did, it's corrupted."

"Damn it." The doctor was more annoyed than worried. "Okay. Have Laverne call the patient back, give them some pretext." She looked sternly at Randall, added, "We'll examine her, see what she remembers."

* * *

The racket from the house shook the very air, rattling the dead panes of black glass that divided the white walls. It was as though machinery whirling inside was imbalanced, running amok like a herd of frenzied washing machines. Icicles of resinous red hung at the eves, cold, slippery, with ruddy tears splashing from them onto the sickly green ground below. There was dark, oily smoke billowing from the chimney, blotting out the sunless sky, leaving a vivid cross light from the broken horizon. The neat, maniacal rows of low crops in the foreground now came into stark relief, like the bars of a prison cell.

Avery screamed, bolting upright, startling Sage into an adrenaline rush that drove both of their hearts at double time. They lay back down, slowly, and then held each other for several minutes, willing themselves out of panic, speaking in soothing tones and whispered affirmation. Eventually, Avery got out of bed.

"That does it." They were searching for their slippers as they spoke. "I'm calling the doctor. I want to see a shrink!"

"That's probably a good idea, Hon." Sage was getting up, too. "I was starting to wonder if you'd be having nightmares all through our honeymoon." They smiled sweetly, sincerely, always the one for empathy and concern, that was Sage.

* * *

Avery saw the voicemail during lunch, listened to it while munching. "Hi, it's Laverne at Dr. Sondra's office. Listen, we spotted a problem with your order, and we need to check it out. It could cause problems if the lab didn't make the lenses correctly. Please call back to make an appointment."

"Great." Avery said out loud. Then, in undertone, "Better get this done ASAP, so they're back before wedding day."

* * *

Laverne looked at the glasses briefly, then stood. "Follow me." Avery trailed along to the exam room. "Please sit here." She was pointing to the seat before one of the examination machines. Avery sat; Laverne stood by the door. "Sorry about this," she was saying, "but sometimes there's a problem." Laverne seemed a little anxious but made some small talk while they waited.

"So. Are you still having those dreams?"

"Yeah," Avery admitted. "But I called my doctor; they gave me a referral to a psychologist."

It seemed odd, but something about Laverne's manner indicated that she already knew this. "Well, that's unfortunate," she said simply. "I believe I told you to let it go."

It was an odd comment, but conversation was interrupted by the door, which opened to admit Randall and Dr. Sondra. It was the doctor who spoke first.

"Hello…" she looked at the patient file, open in her hand, "Avery." She gave a smile that was probably supposed to look friendly. "Let's talk, shall we?"

Randall had passed behind the row of patient chairs that faced the equipment. He was right behind Avery now. The doctor continued.

"What exactly do you remember from this room?"

"Huh?" This was rapidly getting weird. "What do you mean? That guy," Avery jerked a thumb at Randall, "tested my eyes in here, a few weeks ago."

The doctor looked past Avery to where Randall stood, smiling slightly like there was a barely amusing inside joke between them.

"Do you remember this machine?" She was pointing at the one at which Avery now sat.

"No. Yes…I don't know." Avery started to feel inexplicably nervous, but Dr Sondra's voice was soothing.

"Let's take a look, shall we?" She sat down in the operator's chair. "Go ahead and look through the eyepiece," pausing to assist. "Just keep your chin on the rest. Perfect!"

Peering into the machine, Avery was astonished to see the image of a neat green field, clear blue sky, and a house in the distant center. A white farmhouse, with a red roof. "That's the one from my dream!" Starting to pull back from the machine, Avery felt a hand on the shoulder, preventing escape.

"There now," Randall's soothing tone didn't really help. "It's okay. We're just trying to determine what went wrong, we'll have you fixed up very soon."

"Exactly." Dr. Sondra was speaking softly as well. "Just hold tight. Randall's going to give you a little something." Avery felt the prick of an injection, administered deftly in the neck.

"What the fuck was that?"

"Just think of it as gravy for the brain." Randall said, then added in an undertone, "I always wanted to say that!"

Avery was trying to decide which was more relevant: the raw flush of panic, or the waves of yellow warmth that were beginning to wash over them. The warmth was winning.

"Don't worry." It was Laverne's voice, reverberant, reaching Avery from somewhere near the bottom of a distant cave. "You won't remember any of this."

Voices continued, reaching into the fluffy interior of the patient's head from afar, detached from the corporeal world, disconnected from identity.

"She's ready." Pause. "Roll program."

"Loading..."

Avery could hear the ticking of the machine but could not tell if the sound was real. A minute passed, or maybe three.

"Look at the logs. There's that dip. Her brain is fighting it."

"I can see that. Get rid of the house, bring up the balloon scene."

"Good. The series is flattening. Now load the program again."

Another heavy pause, probably a few minutes longer than the first.

"I'm not sure if it's going to take, Randall. No, it's not. Stop the load. Just wipe her memory of us and delete the house page, the balloon—everything in both of those memory chains."

"Okay, Doc. Deprogramming now."

* * *

Avery woke up to Sage's snoring, moments before alarm time. They got up carefully, like one would with a sleeping cat or a fellow soldier, not to be disturbed before it was their time, their choice, to awaken. Slippers on the ready, robe on the hook, house already warming to the daytime setting, Avery started down the stairs. "Wait," a moment of panic quickly turning to the warm glow of relief, "I almost forgot!" They went back to the bedside, reached down to the nightstand, and turned off the alarm with less than a minute to spare.

"You got a call." Sage shifted in the bed, still mostly asleep. "Um, doctor wondering if you wanted to reschedule."

"Thanks." Avery said, "I don't remember having an appointment," thoughtfully, then turned to go.

"Okay." Sage was starting to drift off again, but added, "You still having those dreams?"

Avery shrugged. "I don't ever remember my dreams."

Once Upon a Time

"We two have paddled in the stream,
from morning sun till dine;
But seas between us broad have roared
since auld lang syne.
And there's a hand my trusty friend!
And give me a hand o' thine!
And we'll take a right good-will draught,
for auld lang syne."

– Robert Burns, "Auld lang syne," 1788

The Two Hedgehogs

For Mitch Tiner (10/31/1964 – 1/28/2021)

Once upon a time, there were two hedgehogs. One was tall, the other was quick, and both enjoyed cooking very much. Quick Hedgehog would share recipes with Tall Hedgehog, who would say things like, "That sounds pretty cool, but I need the measurements if I am going to make it." Tall would bring food to Quick's house, and Quick would say, "This is technically pretty good, but your presentation sucks!"

The two hedgehogs loved each other's company and discovered that they each learned a lot from cooking and eating together. When Quick moved to a city far away, Tall was lost for a time. But not for long. The two hedgehogs compared notes and continued to share their recipes by mail. Both of them knew that this was not just about cooking. Both of them knew that, as long as they each believed in each other, everything would be okay.

Ten years went by. Then another ten years. And then another. In three decades, the two hedgehogs earned a few gray hairs, and had many adventures. Quick became a farmer, because that's what he had always been anyway. Tall became an engineer, for the very same reason. You see, when everything is going to be okay, you will eventually find out what you already are, and you will become that. The two hedgehogs learned this, together, in separate parts of the world.

One day, Tall received a letter from his hedgehog friend. Only it wasn't his friend, it was only a dream of his friend. In Quick's dream, we can see Quick climbing a tree in his back yard, and telling us there are apples, just out of reach, and that he wanted them for a pie. "What kind of pie?" asked Tall Hedgehog. Quick just looked down, smiled, and said, "If I really have to explain, you'll never understand."

Once again, Tall was impressed with Quick's uncanny brilliance, and the farmer's intuition that had always evaded Tall's engineering mind. Tall Hedgehog thought for a moment, then turned around to face the tree Quick had been climbing. Tall Hedgehog started to say, "Apple pie! You want the apples for apple pie!" But even as he opened his mouth, Quick had climbed higher, and higher, and higher—until he had passed the top of the tree and disappeared.

That was the last time we saw Quick. Some of us will wonder if he found the apples (and other ingredients) he needed for his apple pie. For Tall Hedgehog, there remains the neverending questions. How many apples? What kind? What are the measurements for the other ingredients? How can I ever get this right without the colorful creativity of Quick Hedgehog?

But even as we ask these questions, the answers are right at hand. If we learn to believe in someone when they're close to us, we will find that we can still believe in them when they are far away. Even so, if we know someone believes in us in person, we must know that they still believe in us when they're gone.

Thank you for believing in me, Quick Hedgehog.

Warm regards,

Tall Hedgehog